Thoroughbred Legacy
The stakes are high.

Scandal has hit the Preston family and their award-winning Quest Stables. Find out what it will take to return this horse-racing dynasty to the winner's circle!

Available July 2008

#1 *Flirting with Trouble* by Elizabeth Bevarly
Publicist Marnie Roberts has just been handed a PR disaster, one that will bring her face-to-face with the man who walked out of her bed and out of her life eight years ago.

#2 *Biding Her Time* by Wendy Warren
Somehow, Audrey Griffin's motto of "seize the day" has unexpectedly thrown her into the arms of a straitlaced Aussie who doesn't do no-strings-attached. Is Audrey balking at commitment…or simply biding her time?

#3 *Picture of Perfection* by Kristin Gabriel
When Carter Phillips sees an exquisite painting that could be the key to saving his career, he goes after the artist. Will he sacrifice his professional future for a personal one with her?

#4 *Something to Talk About* by Joanne Rock
Widowed single mom Amanda Emory is on the run from her past, but when she meets Quest's trainer she suddenly wants to risk it all…and give everyone something to talk about!

Available September 2008
#5 *Millions To Spare* by Barbara Dunlop
#6 *Courting Disaster* by Kathleen O'Reilly
#7 *Who's Cheatin' Who?* by Maggie Price
#8 *A Lady's Luck* by Ken Casper

Available December 2008
#9 *Darci's Pride* by Jenna Mills
#10 *Breaking Free* by Loreth Anne White
#11 *An Indecent Proposal* by Margot Early
#12 *The Secret Heiress* by Bethany Campbell

Dear Reader,

I always have a lot of fun when I join other authors to write a series, but that fun is doubled when the subject matter is near and dear to my heart. My family tree has *very* deep roots in Kentucky, and I currently live right in horse country. I drive past Thoroughbred farms no matter my destination, because they are literally right up and down the road from me. Our state's slogan is "Unbridled spirit," and the reason for that is obvious to anyone who's ever watched one of those majestic animals run. They are joy personified. Horsified. You know what I mean.

I tried to capture both my affection for Kentucky and my admiration of Thoroughbreds when I wrote *Flirting with Trouble*. And I hope I captured the flavor of Australia, too, for the parts of the book that take place in that wonderful country. Daniel Whittleson is like many horsemen I've encountered in his love for the animal, and he's like many heroes I've created in his love for Marnie Roberts. Marnie, too, was delightful to write, because she embodies the hopes and fears of everywoman and she rises to face those hopes and fears with the same sort of bravery.

Best wishes,

Elizabeth Bevarly

Thoroughbred Legacy

ELIZABETH BEVARLY

Flirting with Trouble

Silhouette® Books

Published by Silhouette Books

America's Publisher of Contemporary Romance

SILHOUETTE BOOKS

ISBN-13: 978-0-373-19914-3
ISBN-10:   0-373-19914-7

FLIRTING WITH TROUBLE

Special thanks and acknowledgment are given to Elizabeth Bevarly for her contribution to the Thoroughbred Legacy series.

Visit Silhouette Special Edition and Thoroughbred Legacy at www.eHarlequin.com.

Printed in U.S.A.

ELIZABETH BEVARLY

is a RITA® Award-nominated author of
more than sixty works of contemporary romance.
Her books regularly appear on the *USA TODAY*
bestseller list and the Waldenbooks bestseller lists for
romance and mass-market paperbacks. Her novel
The Thing About Men hit the *New York Times* extended
bestseller list, as well. Her novels have been published
in more than two dozen languages and three dozen
countries, and there are more than ten million copies
in print worldwide. She currently lives in a small town
in her native Kentucky with her husband and son.
Visit her online at www.elizabethbevarly.com.

For everyone who has roots in the Bluegrass State,
whether homegrown or transplanted.
Unbridled spirit indeed.

Chapter One

As he settled his hand on the corral gate and shot his gaze over virtually miles of white plank fencing that crisscrossed and enclosed Quest Stables, it occurred to Daniel Whittleson that a June morning in Kentucky was about as close to heaven as a man could find. And this was only the first of the month. Sure, the dogwoods and redbuds had stopped blooming by now, but the surly spring weather had mellowed into steady blue skies and balmy breezes, and the smothering heat of July and August was still weeks away. The colts of Quest Stables, where he was senior trainer, were confident and playful by now, and they'd discovered the joys of losing themselves to running. A handful of them were doing that now, at the farthest edge of the pasture beyond the corral.

The elegant, shallow hills of Woodford County were awash in the deep green of the bluegrass, dotted here and there with copses of broad, leafy sugar maples and towering oaks. At not quite 7:00 a.m., the sun had just crested one of those hills, tinting the sky with a mellow pink and orange and spilling a wide trail of luscious gold across the pasture.

There must be something about the curvature of the earth at this latitude that made the sunlight do that, Daniel thought. He'd lived and traveled all over the world, and he'd never seen the land glow the way it did in Kentucky when the sun's rays were at their longest. He ran a work-roughened hand through his hair, noting without much surprise that he was way overdue for a cut. Then he lifted the gate's handle and entered the corral, whistling for the chestnut stallion on the other side. The horse's ears stitched forward as he whinnied his objection to being interrupted in his own enjoyment of the morning, then he obediently, though reluctantly, trotted across the corral to where Daniel stood. The horse, Flirting with Trouble, certainly lived up to his name.

He was a spirited two-year-old Daniel was hoping to whip into shape by next year's Kentucky Derby, but so far, Trouble wasn't cooperating. For now, Daniel worked mostly on winning the animal's trust and forging a bond between them. He was confident Trouble would come around. Eventually. Daniel was a firm believer in the old adage about good things coming to those who waited.

Summer wasn't the busiest time of the year for Thoroughbred trainers, but neither was it in any way slow. This year's Derby and Preakness were over—both won handily by Leopold's Legacy, a Quest Thoroughbred, Daniel thought smugly—but the Belmont Stakes were less than two weeks away. And if things went the way they were supposed to, Leopold's Legacy would take that race, too, making him only the twelfth horse in history to earn the Triple Crown.

Daniel hadn't trained Legacy himself, though. That honor had fallen to Robbie Preston, whose family owned Quest Stables, the first of many major wins the young trainer would doubtless see in his life—provided he got over his impatience and learned to handle the pressures that came with the job. Although Daniel wouldn't be part of the group accompanying the horse to New York, he still had plenty to keep him busy on the farm. Which was good, because he thrived on the extra work. Hell, work was what kept him going. Work was the only thing he knew. Well, work and horses. Those he knew better than he did even a lot of people.

And working with horses—and knowing them well—was in the Whittleson blood. Daniel's father, Sam, was also a trainer, respected throughout the Thoroughbred industry worldwide. Respect for his father had come grudgingly for Daniel, however, and even now was restricted to the man's professional skills. Sam had been so serious about horses when Daniel was a child that it had cost the elder Whittleson his family.

The Australian Sam had abandoned Daniel and his American mother before Daniel started school, and Lois Whittleson had been forced to return to the States and work three jobs to keep their heads above water—until her death when Daniel was only fourteen.

At times he'd been convinced it was more the work than the cancer that had killed his mother. And he'd never quite been able to stop blaming his father for that.

Daniel had gone back to live with Sam in Australia following his mother's death, and it had taken years for the two Whittleson men to start communicating like a father and son—however tenuously. It had taken longer for the two of them to settle on an uneasy truce. Daniel supposed he would always harbor some resentment toward his father for not being around when he'd needed him as a child. But Sam had done his best to make amends to his son.

Daniel knew his father cared for him as much as Sam could. But he also knew his father was a horseman first and father second. As an adult, Daniel understood how that could be. Some people simply weren't cut out to be parents. He was a case in point—as guilty as his father when it came to putting his career before anything else. But unlike his father, Daniel knew better than to start a family—or even get seriously involved with a woman—for that very reason.

Still, he was grateful to Sam for teaching him about horses, the one interest the two of them had in common. Hell, it was their combined passion for Thoroughbreds that had put them on speaking terms and kept them there all these years.

Daniel ran a hand over Trouble's slick mane, his gaze sweeping over what he could see of the thousand acres that made Quest the largest Thoroughbred farm in Kentucky. Although Thomas and Jenna Preston, who owned and operated Quest, kept forty-eight horses of their own, they stabled nearly five hundred. Some of the family's horses were foals and broodmares who'd never raced, or stallions past their racing prime, who were still viable at stud. Others were pacers used in training, or retired horses left to graze and run free and enjoy what was left of their lives in leisure. But the majority of the Preston horses were either working Thoroughbreds or racers in training. Even at that, a major source of Quest's income came from boarding and training and stud fees.

The farm employed scores of people, both full- and part-time. In addition to trainers like Daniel, there were groomers, exercisers, stall muckers, groundskeepers, farmers, maintenance workers and a variety of household help. Daniel had worked at Quest for more than seven years now, having come here as a junior trainer in an effort to rebuild both his career and reputation after a self-inflicted debacle in California at the Del Mar Pacific Classic. That race *should* have been the first major victory of his career as Robbie's recent wins would be for his. Except Daniel had been even younger than Robbie, and the win would have cemented his entrée into the highest echelons of Thoroughbred racing that much earlier.

Unfortunately, Daniel hadn't made it to the track on race day. He'd been sidetracked by a woman he never should have gotten involved with in the first place. Marnie Roberts. A rich, pampered socialite who was light-years removed from both the world he'd grown up in and the world he'd lived in then.

The two of them shouldn't even have been in the same room at that party the week before the race. Daniel hadn't been invited and was only there to deliver a message to the wealthy owner of Little Joe, the horse he'd trained for the race. But as he'd made his way out of the palatial Coronado Hotel, his gaze had lit on Marnie's—and hers had lit on his—and the proverbial sparks had flown. They'd chatted for less than half an hour before deciding to blow the joint and get a drink someplace quiet and secluded.

In the week that followed, Daniel had spent far more time with Marnie than he should have. And those times he *was* working with Little Joe, he'd been far too preoccupied by thoughts of Marnie to do his job well. The two of them were explosive together. Their combined chemistry had created a reaction that was nothing short of atomic. And although it had ended up being a week of exceptionally good times—and staggeringly good sex—it had ended in the biggest disaster of Daniel's life. He'd given so much of himself to Marnie that week that there had been nothing left for anything else. Including the race for which he'd come to San Diego in the first place. The night before the

Pacific Classic, he and Marnie had both turned off their cell phones to focus on each other, and after hours of exhaustive, white-hot sex, they'd overslept the next day and Daniel hadn't made it to the track in time for the one o'clock race.

His absence that day—hell, that whole week—had made Little Joe's owner and jockey anxious enough that their anxiety spilled over onto the horse. Little Joe was more restless than usual by race time, and that unease had only been compounded at the starting gate. The horse had lunged and hurt both himself and his jockey, then, after the starting bell, had bolted from the gate, out of control. Ultimately, the horse that all the track insiders were predicting would carry the win by at least a length had come in eighth instead. And it never would have happened if Daniel had been on the job that week, the way he was supposed to be, instead of with Marnie.

He hadn't just lost his job that day. He'd also lost his confidence, his faith in his abilities and his self-respect. He didn't blame Marnie for what had happened. He'd known then—as he knew now—that he had only himself to blame. And he wasn't proud of how he'd behaved in the wake of the disaster where Marnie was concerned. He'd left San Diego that very night, tucking a letter into her mailbox on his way out that told her he'd had to choose between her and his career, and his career had won. He'd been too big a coward to tell her to her face, because whenever he was with Marnie, he couldn't think straight. Had he tried to tell her in person, Marnie would have won over his career. And he would have lost himself to her forever.

Which might not have been so bad, except that high-society party girls like Marnie Roberts didn't stay interested in unemployed losers like Daniel Whittleson. And once Marnie walked out on him—as she would have eventually—he'd be facing both financial *and* emotional poverty.

Still, Daniel had learned a very valuable lesson from the Del Mar experience. He'd learned that he couldn't afford to be sidetracked by things like staggeringly good sex—or even what might have turned out to be a halfway decent, if temporary, relationship with a woman. Work came first for Whittleson men. Especially Daniel. Because work led to success, and success was the only way to escape the insecurity and poverty he'd known as a child.

So Daniel had cut ties with Marnie completely. And he'd stopped thinking about Del Mar and anything related to that sorry chapter of his life a long time ago.

At least until this morning.

He grimaced at the memories and pushed them back into the furthest, darkest, least-visited corner of his brain where they belonged. It hadn't been easy, but he had successfully rebuilt his career after Del Mar, and he would never go back again. He'd practically been a kid with Little Joe, barely out of college with the first horse he'd trained by himself. Now, at thirty-two, he had trained scores of horses, many of whom had gone on to become champions. He was building the pedigree necessary for a trainer who someday intended to own and operate his own stables. Stables that would be successful enough for him to finally reassure the child who still lived inside him fearing poverty and loss. Only when Daniel had achieved that goal would he be able to call himself successful. Only then would he be fulfilled. Personally and professionally. Nothing—nothing in the world—mattered to him more.

"Daniel!"

At the sound of his name, he turned and saw Jenna Preston striding down the steps of the big house, waving her arm over her head to get his attention. The house was a huge, rambling red brick structure, two proud stories of more than five thousand square feet of living space. The front boasted a broad, shady porch supported by pillars, but here in the back, the long, sheltered veranda was less formal. There were two other verandas. The one on the west had comfortable dark green wicker furniture with floral cushions for viewing sunsets, while the east veranda had bamboo furniture for outdoor dining.

Off the east veranda was a cobbled patio with a massive built-in grill and rotisserie, Thomas Preston's pride and joy during the summer months, when he loved to cook for friends and family. Daniel could see the big, kidney-shaped pool shimmering nearby in the morning sun, its deck a tile mosaic of horse-themed images and icons.

A handful of small, tidy cabins were used to house guests and employees—Daniel included—all scattered within easy walk of the big house. Bunkhouses provided lodging for those who worked the farm, and there were barns for the horses, corrals for exercising, a practice track and several storage sheds. In many ways, Quest Stables was like a small town. During busy times of the year, Daniel had been known to go weeks without ever leaving the grounds.

He exited the corral and began to walk in Jenna's direction, meeting her halfway. Like him, she'd been up before the sun and was dressed for the day ahead in blue jeans and work boots and a gray work shirt decorated with the logo of Quest Stables. At fifty-five, Jenna was as trim and fit as life on a working horse farm could make a person. She was a good head shorter than Daniel's own six feet, her auburn hair framing her round face in soft waves. Her cheerful, thoughtful nature was the perfect complement to her husband's straightforward, uncompromising one. Jenna could and did show Thomas sides of a situation he wouldn't bother to entertain himself.

Rumor on the farm had it that not a blade of bluegrass could bend anywhere on the property without Jenna knowing about it. Although she had raised three kids into admirable adults, she still took a maternal interest in some of the younger workers on the farm. Daniel had been one of them when he'd first come to work here. In a lot of ways, Jenna had been the mother he'd lost when he was a teenager.

"Daniel, there's a phone call for you at the big

house," she called when she was within earshot. "They said they tried your cell phone but didn't get an answer."

That was because he never turned on his phone until after he'd enjoyed those few stolen moments at the beginning of the day. He frowned. "It's barely 7:00 a.m. Who is it?"

Her already concerned expression darkened. "They wouldn't say. The caller ID has an international code, though. Australia. And the voice is too official-sounding for them to be calling about something casual."

Daniel's first thought was Sam. "It's not my dad?"

She shook her head.

Her concern infected him then. If it wasn't his dad, there was a strong chance it was about his dad. The old man was only sixty-one and had always been in good health, but that was an age where problems could start showing up. Daniel quickened his pace as he headed for the house, not waiting for Jenna. He took the steps of the veranda by twos and saw the library door—the one through which she must have exited—open. Sure enough, the phone lay on its side on the table nearest the door, so he scooped it up.

"Daniel Whittleson," he said without preamble, barely winded from the brisk walk.

"Mr. Whittleson, this is Detective Headley of the Pepper Flats Police Department."

Something seized Daniel's heart and squeezed hard. Pepper Flats was the town closest to Whittleson Stud, his father's four-hundred-acre station in Hunter Valley, Australia. A call from the police couldn't be good.

The detective's voice was noticeably quieter when he added, "I'm afraid I have a bit of bad news for you, sir."

"What is it?" Daniel could barely get the question out.

"Your father is Samuel Whittleson of Hunter Valley?"

A knot of something hot and sharp tightened in his belly. "Yes," he told the detective. "I'm Sam's son."

There was a slight hesitation, then, "I'm afraid your father's been shot."

"Shot?" Daniel echoed incredulously. Of all the things cartwheeling through his head, a shooting had been nowhere among them.

Before he could say anything else, the detective hurried on. "He's in hospital right now and has an excellent chance of recovery. He was shot in the chest, but the bullet exited cleanly and no vital organs were affected. He may be a while in surgery, though."

Daniel's head was still buzzing with the news that his father had been shot and he barely heard anything else the detective said.

"Do the police have the shooter?" he asked after a moment.

"We do," the detective told him. "Your father was shot by a neighbor, Louisa Fairchild."

It was a name Daniel knew well. Not a conversation with his father went by without Sam saying something about Louisa. The two of them had been feuding over the rights to a lake that adjoined their properties since the day Sam took ownership of his farm a decade ago. Daniel had met the woman a time or two during his visits to his father, and as cantankerous as she was, no way would he have figured her to be capable of shooting someone. Hell, she must be eighty years old!

"Louisa Fairchild?" he echoed. "I'm sorry, but I don't understand. How could Louisa have shot my father?"

There was a meaningful hesitation, then the detective said, "We're still interrogating Miss Fairchild, but she claims it was self-defense."

"What?" Daniel was incredulous. Self-defense indicated that she'd needed to protect herself from Sam Whittleson. And although his father wasn't the most even-tempered, jovial man on the planet, he was in no way abusive.

"I'm afraid, Mr. Whittleson," the detective said, "that there are some mitigating circumstances, and that much of what Miss Fairchild has said isn't quite connecting. We won't have a chance to speak to your father until the doctors give us the go-ahead, which could be days from now. I'm afraid it may be some time before we have the whole story."

Daniel gripped the phone fiercely, his head spinning with all he'd heard, little of which made any sense. One thing, however, was certain. "I can be in Australia tomorrow."

Marnie Roberts was *not* having a good day. She'd awoken to discover that the old song about it never raining in Southern California was a total lie. In fact, there were actual monsoons in Southern California, as evidenced by the puddles of water that had formed beneath the jalousie windows of her San Diego condo during the night. *Inside* the windows, that is. Outside the windows, she'd discovered upon cranking them open and peeping through, someone had evidently moved the condo swimming pool just beneath her unit. Which might have brought up the value of the place if it weren't for the fact that this new pool was filled with muddy water and dead, mushy marigolds.

Things had only gotten worse.

The monsoon had blown out her power, too. So she'd woken up late, with coffee to chase the cobwebs from her brain, no blow-dryer or straightening iron to tame her mass of unruly auburn curls, no steamer to tame her even more unruly clothes, and no light in her window-less bathroom to help her apply her makeup. Conse-quently, when she finally arrived at the San Diego office of Division International Consulting—the PR firm that had employed her for the past five years—she looked nothing like her usual flawlessly professional self. Instead, she looked like…

Well, there was no avoiding it. With her auburn hair lank and lifeless and her butter-yellow business suit wrinkled and limp, she looked like a dead, mushy marigold.

She hated days like this.

Great, she thought as she entered the outer office and breathlessly greeted Phoebe, The Perkiest Recep-tionist in the Pacific Time Zone. This was just great. And today, Marnie was supposed to be meeting with a new client, a rising young comedian who was notorious for cruelly insulting perfectly nice people like, well, like Marnie, and the dead, mushy marigold look was going to give him tons of ammunition.

She really hated days like this.

In an effort to kick her office door closed with one foot, she inadvertently got her heel caught in the carpet and stumbled forward, losing her grip on the mondo-size latte she'd picked up at the drive-through and sending it careening through the air. It landed upside down—naturally—and the plastic top came popping off—inevitably—spilling a river of tan along the pastel dhurrie rug she'd bought for her office only days before—of course. All this after it had sloshed a nice long estuary across the lower portion of her previously butter-yellow suit first.

She really, *really* hated days like this.

She tugged her foot free from the door and slammed it down with confidence—it was *not* petulance—something that made the heel snap off and go flying toward her other calf, leaving a long scrape. Not sure whether she should focus her immediate attention on the shoe, the calf or the rug, she hobbled to her desk and was reaching for a tissue when the intercom buzzed with enough volume to make her squeal.

"Marnie, I need to see you right away," her boss Hildy's voice boomed ominously into the room. Not that Hildy Emerson wasn't ominous and booming every day, but today, she sounded even more urgent than usual.

Not a good sign, Marnie thought. But then, considering how her day had been so far, not exactly surprising, either.

She pushed the button on her intercom. "I'll be right there, Hildy." To herself, she added, Just as soon as I'm presentable. Which should be sometime in September.

As if reading her thoughts, Hildy immediately replied, "I need you *now*."

With a wistful look at the rapidly spreading coffee stain, Marnie scooped up her now-empty cup and still-broken heel and made her way to the door. She dropped the cup in the trash on her way out, then staggered as well as she could to Hildy's office on the other side of the reception area. Phoebe smiled perkily at her as she went, as oblivious to Marnie's plight as she was to anything that wasn't, well, perky. Inhaling a deep, fortifying breath, Marnie turned the knob to Hildy's door and stepped inside.

"Marnie, I—" Her boss stopped cold when she glanced up from the papers on her desk to look at Marnie full on. She assessed Marnie critically from the hair bomb to the stained suit to the broken heel and back again. "My God, what happened to you?"

Marnie sighed, knowing they'd be there all day if she started listing. So she only said, "It does, too, rain in Southern California."

Hildy studied Marnie through narrowed gray eyes.

She opened her mouth as if she intended to ask something else, evidently thought better of it, and gestured toward one of two leather chairs on the other side of her desk. "Have a seat."

Marnie hobbled across the room and folded herself gratefully into the chair, trying not to notice that Hildy's silver-streaked black hair was perfectly coiffed and her plum-colored suit flawless. Hildy was always perfectly coiffed and flawless. That was why she was the employer and Marnie was a coffee-stained employee. As she sat in the chair indicated, she toed off her broken shoe and began trying to work the heel back on.

"You need to drop every account you have right now," Hildy told her, "and focus on a new assignment."

"Whoa, whoa, whoa," Marnie objected immediately, her broken heel forgotten. "I'm juggling more than a dozen clients right now, on three continents. I can't just blow them all off. They'll—"

"Someone else can handle them," Hildy interrupted. "I need you for something big."

"Oh, bigger than Prince Torquil?" Marnie asked indignantly, citing the assignment that Hildy had previously told her should take precedence over everything else.

"This is much worse than Prince Torquil," Hildy said evenly.

"I don't see how it could be," Marnie replied. "I mean, the Tortugan officials won't even let King Bardo and Queen Ingeborg bring Torquil a minibar *or* personal chef to the jail. From all accounts, it's been ugly."

Now Hildy made a face. "Torquil will survive. We'll let Jerry Turner handle it. He has a winter home down there somewhere. It'll be like a paid vacation for him."

Marnie started to object again, but was halted by Hildy's raised hand.

"Louisa Fairchild has shot someone," her boss told her.

Marnie's mouth fell open and the forgotten shoe heel tumbled completely from her hand. Though, honestly, she didn't know why she should be surprised. Louisa Fairchild was one of Division's most crotchety clients, even living half a world away in Australia. One of their newer clients, she'd zoomed straight to the top of their list of High Maintenance Accounts. Even Prince Torquil's martini deprivation paled in comparison. But then, Louisa Fairchild's level of difficulty was pretty legendary, extending beyond the Thoroughbred industry in which she was practically an icon. Marnie had heard tales of the grand dame when she was a child, riding dressage herself.

"What happened?" Marnie asked.

Hildy sighed and leaned back in her chair. "It's going to be a mess. Although Louisa claims it was self-defense, there are a number of extenuating circumstances and enough he said–she said to make your brain explode. Still," she added thoughtfully, "the man she shot…Sam somebody…it's all in the file…was in Louisa's house when it happened, purportedly uninvited. Unfortunately, no one can prove he wasn't there by invitation."

"There were no witnesses?" Marnie asked.

Hildy shook her head. "None."

Marnie groaned. "Great. And the annual Fairchild Gala is how far off?"

Hildy's smile was brittle. "Less than two weeks."

Marnie nodded. Hildy was right. Prince Torquil's snafu had nothing on a Louisa Fairchild shooting.

"You're going to have a lot of damage control to do," Hildy told her. "Louisa Fairchild is our first Australian client, and we're working hard to make inroads into that country to broaden our base. And that gala she has is nationally recognized for raising hundreds of thousands of dollars for kids with special needs. If you handle this correctly, the gala will still go off without a hitch. And if Louisa comes out of this looking like the wounded party I'm confident she is, it could be just the ticket we need to expand our clientele."

Oh, hey, no pressure there, Marnie thought. She just wished she was as confident of Louisa's innocence as Hildy was.

Then again, Louisa was an eighty-year-old woman. What kind of man went after an eighty-year-old woman, even a cantankerous one? Of course Louisa Fairchild was the victim in this. Of course she was.

Hildy slid a manila file folder across the desk, which Marnie was confident would have all the information she needed for the case, and quickly began covering the basics. As her boss spoke, Marnie began to flip idly through the pages in the folder, realizing there was too much information to absorb casually. But, hey, that was okay—she'd have plenty of time to study it in depth on the trans-Pacific flight she would doubtless be taking within hours.

As if reading her mind—again—Hildy concluded, "Go home and pack a bag, Marnie. You're on a three o'clock flight to Sydney."

This was the part of the job Marnie hated most. The sudden switching of gears, the travel for which she had no time to prepare. It wasn't unusual in public relations to experience both. Especially for a company like Division International, whose client list was overwhelmingly wealthy, pampered and used to getting their way. Of course, there had been a time in Marnie's life when she herself had been wealthy, pampered and used to getting her way, but those days had come to an end seven years ago, when her father had lost everything—including the trust fund she'd assumed would always be there.

Marnie was about to flip the folder closed when she noticed the name at the bottom of the first page. The name of the man Louisa Fairchild had shot. The man who was, at that very moment, lying in a Sydney hospital undergoing surgery.

Sam Whittleson.

No, Marnie thought, physically shaking her head, as if that might negate what she was seeing. Oh, no. No, no, no, no, no. Not Sam Whittleson. Not *any* Whittleson. Not ever again.

Most especially not Daniel Whittleson. Daniel Whittleson, the only man with whom Marnie had ever come close to falling in love. Daniel Whittleson, who'd come into her life out of nowhere eight years ago and made her rethink everything she'd wanted out of life. Daniel Whittleson, who had been charming and funny and decent and sweet—or so she'd thought—and who had shown her how very good it could be between two people…before dumping her with a Dear Jane letter in which he'd made it clear she was less important to him than the horses that could make him mountains of money. Daniel Whittleson, who had made her feel cherished and loved and important…before breaking her heart in two.

Daniel Whittleson, whose father, Sam, trained horses in Australia.

Chapter Two

"Mr. Whittleson?"

Daniel glanced up from where he sat beside his father's hospital bed. The nurse had spoken his name barely loud enough to hear it. Dressed in the traditional white uniform so many nurses in the States had abandoned in favor of brightly colored scrubs, she looked to be in her fifties and had the sort of soft, pleasant features a person liked to see in someone whose job was taking care of others.

In the same hushed tone, he said, "Yes?"

"I'm sorry to disturb you, but you have a visitor."

"Don't you mean my father has a visitor?"

She shook her head. "No, sir. The woman asked if a Daniel Whittleson was here. That's you, isn't it?"

He nodded. "Yeah, that's me."

But why would anyone be visiting him? he wondered as he rose to follow the nurse out. He didn't know anyone in Hunter Valley besides his father and Sam's handful of friends, all of whom had already called or stopped by to check on him. And he was certain there were no women in his father's life.

"Did she give you a name?" Daniel asked.

"No, she didn't," the nurse told him. She stopped in the middle of the hallway and gestured toward the end. "But she's waiting for you in the waiting room down there."

"Thanks," Daniel said with some distraction as he strode in that direction.

At first, he didn't recognize the sole occupant of the room. She was standing in profile, looking out the windows, staring at the lights of the dark and half-empty parking lot beyond. She was clearly deep in thought and unaware of his arrival, something that only intensified his confusion. He was about to speak when it finally hit him— like a two-by-four to the back of the head—who she was. It was as if thinking about her yesterday had made her suddenly appear today. Except she was supposed to be an ocean—and a lifetime—removed from here.

Marnie Roberts. Good God. What the hell was she doing here?

She had changed in the almost decade since their parting. A lot. Her hair was shorter, and dressed in tailored brown trousers and a shirt the burnt sienna of autumn leaves, she looked less like the vivid, bubbly party girl he remembered and more like a sophisticated career woman. But she'd softened the attire with a necklace and bracelet made of ribbons and beads, a bit of whimsy amid the elegance, and much more in keeping with the girlish flirt fresh out of college that he'd met in San Diego.

The minute she'd breezed into the ballroom of the Coronado Hotel as he was making his way out, Daniel had been smitten. Laughing and walk-dancing in time to the music, she'd been as effervescent as the dewy flute of champagne she'd been holding. He'd watched her as she plucked a chocolate-covered strawberry from a passing waiter and lifted it to her mouth, skimming the treat along her lower lip before taking a delicate bite. As if sensing his scrutiny, she'd glanced up just as she was sinking her teeth into the berry a second time, and her enormous eyes had widened in surprise before sparkling with laughter.

Once she'd realized she had an audience, she'd finished the fruit with an erotic flair. Her eyes never leaving his, she'd flicked the tip of her tongue against the luscious half-eaten berry before dragging it along her lip again, then sucked it softly into her mouth. Daniel had never been more aroused in his life as he watched her, and he hadn't even known her name.

She'd fixed that problem immediately, though, doing the walk-dance thing across the room to boldly introduce herself. Her short, floaty dress was the same dark green color as her eyes, and diamond and emerald solitaires winked from her ears. They'd been triple-pierced, he remembered, and coupled with the dash of silver glitter under each eyebrow, she'd looked like a wild thing bent on mischief. At that point, Daniel had been so stressed out by the upcoming race, he'd decided a little walk on the wild side was exactly what he needed.

He'd had no idea just how long and complicated a trip it would turn out to be.

For the first time since arriving in Australia, he was conscious of his appearance, and he suddenly wished it hadn't been thirty-six hours since he'd showered and shaved and changed into the now-disheveled jeans and oatmeal-colored sweater the Southern Hemisphere winter had demanded. Then he wondered why he cared. Marnie must hate him for the way he'd ended things in San Diego. Yeah, it had been eight years since the two of them had seen each other, and they'd both doubtless changed a lot in that time. But there were some hurts that went too deep, some hurts that people never forgot—regardless of whether they'd been the one who got hurt or the one who did the hurting.

"Marnie?" he said softly.

She turned quickly at the sound of his voice. Her lips parted for a moment, as if she were going to say something, then closed again when no words emerged. She made an effort to smile, but the gesture was clearly forced, and nothing like the smiles he remembered from San Diego, so quick and free and full of spirit.

"Daniel," she finally said, the word coming out quiet and anxious. "How's your father?"

Still befuddled by her sudden appearance, he spoke automatically, telling her what he'd told all of his father's callers and visitors. "He's groggy from his meds and spends most of his time sleeping, but he's going to be okay. The doctor said if his progress is good, he can go home in less than a week."

She nodded, a jerky, nervous gesture. "Good. That's good."

He shook his head slowly, as if that might somehow clear it of the cobwebs that were growing thicker by the moment. Of all the people in the world he might have expected to run into in Pepper Flats, Marnie Roberts wouldn't have made the list. True, the Hunter Valley area rivaled California's Sonoma Valley for tourism, and Pepper Flats was the largest of many small townships in the Upper Hunter Shire. But even though it had been founded in the mid-1800s, fewer than five thousand people called the town home. It was beautiful in warmer months, nestled among parks and nature preserves, and played host to festivals celebrating the local heritage and industries—everything from wine and Thoroughbreds to antiques and crafts. During those greener times, it was a lush, tranquil agricultural region that was home to some of New South Wales's most prominent families.

But it was winter now, so there wasn't much reason to visit. Add to that the fact that Pepper Flats was located two hours north of Sydney, and there was even less reason to come this time of year. For Marnie Roberts, a woman Daniel had last seen on the other side of the world eight years ago, to suddenly appear here out of nowhere…

"Marnie, what are you doing here?" he asked, unable to hide his astonishment.

She stared down at her coffee, silent for a long time. Then she looked up at him again. She opened her mouth to reply, but closed it, her gaze ricocheting off his. Finally, with clear discomfort, she said, "I'm, um, in Hunter Valley on business. I, ah…I read the article in today's paper about Sam being shot and brought here, and I, uh…" She glanced at him again, looking strangely guilty about something, then stared down at her coffee once more. "I just…I figured you might be here, and that, ah…you know…you might welcome a familiar face."

She looked up at Daniel again, but only held eye contact for a second. "I mean, if it were me, with my dad in the hospital in a strange place, and if someone I knew—even if I hadn't seen them for a long time, and even if that person wasn't a close friend—was in town, I know I'd be grateful to them for stopping by. So I…you know…stopped by."

Wasn't a close friend, Daniel echoed to himself. Was that really the way she felt? That he *wasn't a close friend?* For months after leaving San Diego—after leaving Marnie—he'd worried she loathed him. That he'd hurt her enough that she would never forgive him. And now she was telling him she simply considered him *not a close friend?* Had that week meant so little to her? Had it just been one of many similar weeks she'd enjoyed? Had he been one of many men to briefly share her bed? Had it been that easy for her to consider what had happened just one of those things and move on?

And if so, why did that bother him so much? Hell, hadn't he just been thinking of that week as little more than a walk on the wild side himself? He should be relieved she felt the way she did. It meant she hadn't been hurt deeply by what he'd done.

And why did that bother him even more?

"I know I only met your dad the one time at the track," she continued, glancing up again…and then looking away again. "But I liked him. He was…nice to me."

Funny, but she made it sound as if she were surprised someone would be nice to her. Daniel had gotten the impression that week in San Diego that she had more friends than she knew what to do with. Though, now that he thought about it, she'd never had to cancel any engagements to be with him. But then, that was the way with rich society girls. They didn't worry about who they were standing up, right? But that didn't seem like the Marnie he remembered, either.

He pushed the thoughts away. The less he remembered about that week, the better. "You made a good impression on Dad, too," he said. Without thinking, he added, "That wasn't always the case with the girls I dated."

He winced inwardly after saying it. Not just because he really hadn't wanted to dwell on their time together, but because what he said made it sound as though Marnie had been one in a long line of meaningless women. And that wasn't true at all.

Daniel had been so focused on building his career that he'd seldom gotten involved with *any* women. He'd only meant that Marnie had been the kind of woman a father liked to see his son dating. Beautiful, charming, fun-loving, rich... Sam had told Daniel after meeting Marnie that he'd be a fool to let a girl like that get away. And what had Daniel done? Hell, he'd practically thrown her away. But back then, his budding reputation and career as a trainer had been what he cared about more than anything in the world. And now...

This time he was the one to look away from Marnie. Now, he felt the same way. His career was everything to him. Always had been. Always would be. It had been a long time since he'd felt poor and insignificant and unimportant. A long time since he'd known fear and insecurity and loss. Work had saved him from all those things. Work had given him everything he'd ever wanted, everything he'd needed—social standing, money in the bank, a sense of purpose and belonging. Work would take him exactly where he wanted to go— to that Thoroughbred farm with a powerhouse reputation and his name on the letterhead. Work brought success. And success brought security. Stability. Status. Daniel would never go back to his humble beginnings again.

Never.

"Daniel, why would someone shoot your father?" Marnie asked.

He sighed heavily and scrubbed a hand through his hair, feeling way more tired than a couple of nights without decent sleep should make a man feel. "I'm still not sure about the details myself," he told her. "There are some aspects of the shooting the police aren't willing to discuss, and some that make no sense. And Dad's been too out of it to say much."

"He was shot by a neighbor?" she asked. When he looked at her again, she added, "I mean, um… That was what the article in the paper said."

He moved his hand to the back of his neck to rub at a knot of tension. "Yeah. An elderly woman named Louisa Fairchild. They've been arguing over rights to a lake that joins their properties for a while now, but I never thought it would escalate to something like this. She said it was in self-defense, that my father attacked her in her home. But I just don't believe that. My father would never do something like that. And to make matters worse," he continued, "Louisa Fairchild wants to press charges against the man *she shot,* wants to send my father to jail for assault and trespassing and God knows what else. It's nuts. *She's* nuts. And here I am, wanting an eighty-year-old woman to go to jail, and feeling like a louse about it."

"Surely everything can be straightened out," Marnie said.

He gaped at her. "Straightened out? The woman tried

to kill my father, Marnie. The only way this will get *straightened out* is if my father fully recovers, and she pays for her crime."

"Daniel, I didn't mean…" Marnie sighed, sounding as weary as he was. "I'm sorry. I didn't mean for that to sound flippant. I'm sure everything will work out all right. What's most important is that your father is going to be okay."

"True," Daniel agreed. "But I want Louisa Fairchild to pay for what she did, and I want her to stop trying to make my father out to be a criminal. The shooting was totally unprovoked. The woman is clearly crazy. But she's adamant that the police arrest my father as soon as he's coherent enough to understand the charges against him. And they haven't ruled that out yet."

Marnie opened her mouth to say something else, evidently thought better of it, and closed it again. But her expression was one of obvious distress, and Daniel immediately felt guilty for jumping down her throat.

"Look, you don't have to apologize," he said. "I'm the one who should apologize. I shouldn't have gone off the way I did. That was uncalled-for."

"It's okay," she told him. "I don't blame you for feeling the way you do. I just…"

"What?" he asked.

But she only shook her head and left that statement unfinished, too.

Daniel sighed again. "I'm sorry," he said, more calmly this time. "I'm just worried about my dad, and

I haven't gotten much sleep since the police called me, and the trip from Kentucky was grueling."

Her lips parted in a little half smile at that, and she seemed to relax at the change of subject. "You're living in Kentucky now?"

He nodded, equally grateful for another topic, if for no other reason than it took his mind off his father for a few minutes. "In Woodford County. I'm the senior trainer for Quest Stables. It's owned by—"

"Jenna and Thomas Preston," she finished for him.

The fact she knew surprised him. "You're familiar with it?"

"Anyone who's ever worked with horses is familiar with it," she told him. "Maybe I wasn't raised around Thoroughbreds, but the equestrian world isn't exactly a big one."

He eyed her intently. "I didn't think you rode anymore."

She eyed him back just as interestedly. "How did you know that?"

Oh, hell. He knew that because he'd met a woman a year or so after Del Mar who'd remembered encountering Daniel and Marnie at a restaurant there, and had remarked what a cute couple the two had made. She'd turned out to be a friend of Marnie's mother and had mentioned that Marnie had given up riding, not just competitively, but completely. Daniel had never discovered why, because he'd manufactured an excuse to extract himself from the conversation before the woman could fill him in on any more about Marnie's life. He'd finally reached a point by then where he wasn't thinking about her every day and hadn't wanted to lose ground.

For now, though, he only said, "I ran into a friend of your mother's at a party in Ocala a while back, and she mentioned it."

Marnie nodded, but didn't seem to want to revisit the past any more than he did. She continued, rather hastily, "Not to mention Quest is the home of Leopold's Legacy, who's about to win the Triple Crown. And with a woman jockey, no less. But you didn't train him," she added, sounding a little surprised at that.

Maybe she didn't ride anymore, but it was obvious she was still interested in the horse world. He shook his head. "No, the Prestons' son Robbie trained Legacy."

"Leopold's Legacy is all over the news with the Belmont Stakes so close. I would have known where you were if I'd heard you were his trainer."

And why did she sound as if she might have liked to know where he was? More to the point, why did it make him feel kind of good to think that might be the case?

Lack of sleep, he told himself. It did funny things to a person.

Which must have been the only reason he heard himself say, "Dad's sleeping, and I haven't eaten anything since this afternoon. Do you want to go down to the coffee shop and grab a late dinner?"

What the hell was he doing? Inviting Marnie to get a bite to eat? Thinking she'd actually accept him? Forget sleep deprivation. He was suffering from sleep delusion.

Or maybe it was just as she'd said—that he was grateful to see a familiar face when he was going through such a stressful situation so far from home.

Incredibly, Marnie didn't decline the invitation. She seemed about to, then, suddenly, she smiled. A smile that was equal parts happiness and melancholy, hope and regret. It was less the smile of the happy-go-lucky girl he'd known in San Diego, and more the smile of a wiser, more seasoned woman.

Finally, she said, "I haven't had dinner yet, either. A bite to eat sounds good."

What the hell was she doing?

As Marnie strode with Daniel through the halls of Elias Memorial Hospital, she asked herself that question and a dozen others. Why was she being so nice to him after the way he'd left her in Del Mar? Where was the outrage she was supposed to be feeling for the man who had dumped her? Why was she genuinely curious about what he'd been doing for the past eight years? Why didn't she hate him? But hovering above all those questions was an even more important one: Why hadn't she told him yet her real reason for being here?

She'd had hours on the plane between San Diego and Sydney to think about their upcoming meeting. But as she'd tried to figure out how she felt about Daniel Whittleson now and plan their inevitable meeting accordingly, she'd been inundated by memories of the past. When she'd finally landed in Australia, she'd had no plan of attack and felt more confused than when she'd left home.

Ultimately, she'd been forced to admit that she didn't know how she felt about Daniel Whittleson now. She wasn't the same person she'd been eight years ago. So much had happened since the last time she saw him, things that had changed her very core. Her father's business had failed less than a year after her week with Daniel, something that had sent her family into a tailspin. Virtually overnight, Marnie had gone from rich to poor, from frivolous to serious, from party girl to working girl. There had been times during the trans-Pacific flight when she'd felt as if she didn't know Daniel Whittleson at all. Not as the Marnie Roberts she was now.

After he'd left San Diego, she'd told herself that if she ever ran into him again, she'd be civil but cool. Show him that she'd put the past behind her and moved on, but that she didn't quite forgive him for what he'd done. Instead, tonight, she'd been nervous and uncertain…and accommodating. She'd even accepted an invitation to join him for dinner. What was the matter with her?

But more important than any of that, she still hadn't told him the reason she was in Hunter Valley. That was, after all, why she'd gone to the hospital. That and to inquire about Sam's condition. She may have been unsure about many things with regard to Daniel, but there had been one decision she *had* made on the flight—to tell him immediately that she was working for Louisa Fairchild. And she'd thought it might be easier to talk to him if she went to see him as Marnie Roberts, an old acquaintance—for lack of a better word—instead of Marnie Roberts, representative of Division International, working on behalf of the woman who'd shot his father. She'd thought he might be more likely to listen to what she had to say in a less-confrontational atmosphere like the hospital than an office environment, or even his father's house.

She'd worried, too, that Daniel wouldn't agree to see her if she tried to set up an appointment as Louisa's representative. And all right, she'd also thought that maybe by catching him off guard, he might be more amenable to a dialogue about the shooting that didn't involve criminal charges.

What she *hadn't* thought was that seeing him again would rouse all those old feelings from eight years ago. And not the bad ones like her turmoil at his panicked departure from her condo when he realized he was late for the race. Or, worse, the sickness that overcame her when she found his letter in her mailbox that evening after returning from the track to look for him—and not finding him. Those were the memories that should have risen most quickly, because those were the ones that had hurt so much.

Instead, she was remembering the good parts of that week. Like strolling hand in hand along Moonlight Beach in Encinitas. And tooling along Harbor Drive in her convertible with the top down. And licking the churro sugar from each other's fingers on the patio at Café Coyote.

Then again, she thought as the images unrolled in her mind, thinking about those things now hurt even more than the memories of Daniel's leaving did....

Oh, God. Just when she'd been feeling as though her life was finally settling down after years of struggle, why did Daniel have to walk back into it? He'd been the first of many things to go wrong eight years ago, and having him come back now made her feel as if she were going in circles, as if the bad times were just looping around to start over again. Only this time, she and Daniel weren't two strangers meeting to embark on a week full of lovely experiences. This time, they were on opposite sides in a volatile situation that was bound to create bad feelings.

And this time, there wouldn't be a second chance eight years down the road to meet and talk and perhaps find closure. Because after what Marnie was going to have to do, Daniel would never want to look at her again.

Chapter Three

After placing their order in the café, Marnie studied Daniel from the other side of the table and tried to figure out how to tell him she was representing Louisa.

Oh, hi, Daniel. Great to see you after all these years of not knowing where you were or what you were doing after you dumped me. But, listen, here's the thing. It's kind of a funny story, actually. That woman who shot and nearly killed your father? The one who wants to send him to jail? I'm supposed to make her come out smelling like a rose and see that your father is the one who ends up looking like the criminal. So how the hell are ya?

Somehow, saying something like that just didn't seem like good PR.

Technically, she thought, she hadn't lied to him. She

was in Hunter Valley on business, and she *had* read about Sam's shooting in the newspaper. In fact, everything she'd said to Daniel tonight had been true. It just hadn't been exactly straightforward.

But, hey, he hadn't exactly been straightforward with her eight years ago, had he? After spending a wonderful week together, he'd pretty much told her she mattered less to him than his horses. And in that same week, she'd begun to feel like Daniel Whittleson might just be The One. Her response to him was so much stronger than with other men. Other men with whom she'd spent significantly more time. She and Daniel had felt good together. They'd felt right. She'd been so sure he shared those feelings. The way he had looked at her. The things he'd said. The way he'd made her feel...

And seeing him again, Marnie realized she'd never quite stopped feeling those things for him. If she didn't think about the way their time together had ended, she could almost imagine it was eight years ago, and the two of them were back at her condo on the beach, laughing and feeding each other shrimp and sharing the last bottle of beer in her refrigerator.

Except that Daniel didn't look like the young, up-and-coming trainer she remembered from back then. Eight years had woven a few threads of silver into his black hair and carved faint lines around his espresso-colored eyes. Eight years had toughened his complexion to a rich bronze and roughened his hands deliciously. The years had broadened his shoulders and roped the muscles of his forearms where he'd pushed up the sleeves of his sweater. She wasn't sure, but he seemed an inch or two taller, because she didn't recall him being quite so... overwhelming.

A ribbon of something hot and electric uncurled in her belly as she looked at him, but it wasn't the same heat and electricity she remembered from San Diego. She'd wanted Daniel with a young girl's desire back then, all urgent and needy and intense. Looking at him now, she felt desire kindling again, but it was different this time. It went deeper and pulled harder and somehow felt even stronger than it had before.

How could that be? she wondered. How could she still want him? She told herself she was remembering an idealized version of him and all the good times they'd had, conveniently forgetting the very real hurt he'd left her with.

She gave herself a good mental shake. Daniel Whittleson had abandoned her. He'd hurt her. When didn't matter. He couldn't be trusted. Even if she forgave him for what had happened in San Diego—and she wasn't sure she had—chances were good he hadn't changed. If she didn't remember anything else, she told herself, she'd damned well better remember that.

Still, she couldn't deny that the years had wrought more than physical changes in him. He didn't smile the same way he had then. Granted, he must have had the scare of his life finding out his father was shot. But it was more than that. There was a caution in him now that she sensed had been there for some time. And the wariness in his eyes when he looked at her hadn't been there before. As if he wasn't sure he could trust her.

Then again, she thought, he *couldn't* trust her. Because she wasn't being honest with him.

Straightforward, she corrected herself. She just wasn't being straightforward.

"So what kind of work brought you to Hunter Valley?" he asked after the waitress brought their coffee. His voice still bore that trace of an accent she remembered. Not quite Australian, not quite English, not quite American, either. It was a mix of all the places he'd lived and worked, something that made him seem slightly exotic.

She chose her words carefully. "I work for Division International. It's a San Diego PR firm." There. That much was true.

He looked puzzled. "Public relations?"

She nodded, but didn't elaborate.

"But your degree is in business. You told me you wanted to run an equestrian camp for at-risk kids. Take them out of depressed urban areas and put them in the countryside where they could get sunshine and fresh air and learn to ride. You said you had some trust fund money you were going to use for the start-up."

She curled her fingers around her coffee mug, suddenly feeling a little chilly inside. "That was a long time ago," she told him.

"It wasn't that long."

"Yeah, Daniel, it was."

A lifetime ago, she thought to herself. Back when she'd been happy and felt fortunate and wanted to share that happiness and good fortune with the rest of the world.

"What happened to change your mind?" he asked.

She sighed. "Not long after you... Not long after San Diego," she quickly amended, "my father's business failed. We lost everything."

Daniel lowered his coffee cup. "Everything?" he asked.

"Everything," she told him. She glanced up to meet his gaze, found that she couldn't hold it, and looked back down. "To pay Dad's creditors and survive the financial loss, we had to liquidate everything. Including my trust fund, my car and Blue Boy."

"Your horse," he said.

She nodded.

"But you really loved that horse."

"I did," she agreed. "But he was worth more than twenty thousand dollars, so..."

"He had to be liquidated," he finished for her.

"Yeah." She tried to smile. "He was bought by a very nice man, though, as a gift for his daughter's tenth birthday. So Blue Boy ended up with a little girl who loved him. And he loved kids."

"He wasn't with you, though."

"No, he wasn't."

Daniel said nothing for a moment. "You had to give up a lot when your father lost his business."

Marnie nodded. "Yeah, but losing Blue Boy was the worst of it."

"You sure about that?"

"Totally."

"No more big house or fancy convertible," he reminded her.

"No."

"No more condo on the beach."

"No."

"No more life of leisure."

As if she'd ever really enjoyed that anyway, Marnie thought. "No."

"No more dreams of equestrian camp."

"No," she said sadly. "Which was the second-worst thing to lose."

He was silent again, and she suddenly wished like hell she knew what he was thinking.

"Well, at least you still had your friends," he said.

"Yeah, at least I had that." Hardly. It was amazing how quickly people abandoned a person when she hit a rough patch. Of course, Marnie supposed she could argue that if they'd abandoned her when she really needed them, they weren't friends in the first place.

And really, she didn't miss them. Not anymore. It had been difficult at first. Terrifying, actually. She and her parents had felt dazed and displaced and wondered if anything would ever feel normal again. But her father had emerged from bankruptcy with a newfound sense of purpose and, with help from friends who invested with him, started a new business from scratch. It was significantly smaller in nature than his previous one had been, but he was enjoying himself more. Her mother had become his assistant in running the small vineyard they'd purchased three years ago. It would be turning a profit for the first time this year, a very modest one, and Marnie hadn't seen her parents so happy in a long time. In many ways, they seemed happier now than they'd been when they were on society's A-list.

Marnie, too, had found some small degree of happiness after losing everything. No, she wasn't following the dream she'd originally mapped out for herself, and there were times when her job drove her crazy. But she'd convinced Hildy at Division to take on a handful of small accounts that weren't as profitable to the company but were still worthwhile—like her parents' business—and she enjoyed working with them. The big fish on Division's client list might be the ones who paid Marnie's salary, but it was the small fish who brought her satisfaction. Maybe someday she'd have her own PR firm and work with causes she considered worthy. And maybe then, she'd be as happy as her parents were.

"I know public relations might seem like kind of a strange occupation for me," she said now, "but it's actually a good fit. I like people, and Division liked the fact that I knew so many, some of them very prominent. I've been doing it for more than five years now." She sat up and lifted her chin a little defiantly as she added, "And I'm good at it, too."

"I don't doubt it for a minute," Daniel said. "I'm sure you could do whatever you put your mind to."

"Thank you."

"It's just that you seemed so focused on the camp for kids, that's all."

Marnie really didn't want to talk about this right now. So she said, "It's good to see you again, Daniel."

Oh, damn, where had that come from? She really hadn't meant to say anything like that. She really hadn't meant to *feel* anything like that. But she'd be lying if she didn't admit that she was still attracted to Daniel. The moment she'd turned to see him in the waiting room, her heart had begun to hammer, and heat had pooled low in her belly. And when he'd uttered her name in that low, soft way he used to… When she looked at his hands and remembered what they had felt like skimming over her bare skin… When she looked at his mouth and recalled the way he'd kissed her and tasted her, and all the places he'd kissed and tasted…

She halted the memories from forming, but not before they ratcheted up her body temperature a few degrees. Daniel Whittleson had been an incredible lover, had scorched her with his touch and enflamed her with his words, until she'd been unable to think about anything but him, until she could only feel him surrounding her and burying himself inside her, and…

She closed her eyes, hoping to put an end to both her distant memories and her current desires. There was no way she could allow herself to be attracted to Daniel again. It would mean risking her heart all over again, and then there was the difficult position her job had put her in.

But when she opened her eyes again, her resolve was nearly shattered. Because Daniel was looking at her as if he felt the same pull from the past that she did, as if he were remembering the same things she was remembering, as if he wanted and needed her now as much as he had then.

Very softly, he replied, "It's good to see you, too, Marnie."

And something inside her broke open, releasing all the feelings she'd wanted so desperately to keep locked up tight.

Oh, Daniel, she thought. Why did we have to meet again now? Why here?

She searched for something, anything, to say that might dispel the almost palpable awareness that lay between them. But all she could come up with was a very lame, "So. You, uh…you work for the Prestons. That must be interesting. They've bred and trained some pretty amazing horses."

At first, she feared he would only continue to look at her with that same soulful yearning she felt so keenly herself. Finally, though, he nodded and said, "I like it very much, actually. Thomas and Jenna are good people. The whole family is." He was thoughtful a moment, as if he still wanted to talk about himself and Marnie, then, thankfully, added, "Their son Andrew has taken over as business manager of Quest. Their son Brent is head breeder. Robbie's turning out to be a top-notch trainer after years of Jenna and Thomas worrying he'd never figure out what he wanted to do with his life. And Melanie just made history as the first female jockey to win the Kentucky Derby *and* the Preakness. Quest Stables is a wonderful place to work. And Kentucky's a gorgeous state."

Marnie forced a smile she hoped looked genuine. "I imagine it's very different from some of the other places you've lived. I mean, a guy who followed his dad to jobs in Australia and England and Canada when he was a teenager, settling in a quiet state like Kentucky? Who would've guessed?"

"It's different from those places in some ways, yeah," he agreed. "But I like it as well or better than any of them." He hesitated a moment before adding, "Though it always feels good to come back to Australia. I was born here, even if I moved back to Ohio with my mom before I started school, so I guess, technically, it's home."

They spent the next hour in companionable conversation, only skimming the surface of whatever they might actually be thinking or feeling, at least on Marnie's part. But she was grateful for it. For now, at least, they both seemed willing to let whatever lay in the past stay there. She'd worry about the future when it came. And she'd worry about the past some other time. For this evening, she was content to just reacquaint herself with Daniel. Even if it was only superficially. And even if it wouldn't last.

Gosh, just like old times.

After finishing dinner, they returned to Sam's hospital room to check on him, but he'd just been given a sedative and the nurse said he was expected to sleep through the night with no change. Daniel double-checked to be sure the hospital had his cell number, then said he'd be at his father's house if there were any developments.

He turned to Marnie. "Where are you staying?"

"I'm staying here in Pepper Flats, actually," she said. "At the Wallaroo Inn."

"How long will you be in town?"

Not an easy question to answer, Marnie thought— honestly *or* dishon…uh, not straightforwardly. As long as it took to clear Louisa's name and ensure that the Fairchild Gala went off without a hitch. Hopefully, that wouldn't take long. But how was Marnie supposed to answer him honestly without revealing the nature of her job? And why was she putting off telling him when he was bound to find out anyway? Especially since his question provided her with a perfect opening?

"I…" She hesitated a moment, telling herself to just spit out the truth and be done with it. Instead, she heard herself say, "Not long."

And she hoped like hell that Louisa did what Marnie told her to do so they could put this all behind them and Marnie could go back to San Diego. Otherwise, she'd just told Daniel a lie. The only lie she'd ever told him, and she hoped it was the last one.

"I'm staying at my dad's place," he said. "He has a spread called Whittleson Stud about a half hour from here. Can I give you a lift back to the hotel? Or do you have a car?"

"I have a car," she told him. "But I took a cab to the hospital because I didn't want to have to navigate the town my first night here after such a long flight."

He looked at her with surprise, and at first, she didn't know why.

"You just got here today?"

She nodded reluctantly.

"And you came to the hospital before doing anything else?"

She nodded again, even more reluctantly. He was going to think there was something suspicious about that.

Instead, he smiled and that ribbon of heat unfurled in her once more. But it was replaced by guilt when he added, "That was nice of you, Marnie. I didn't realize you thought so highly of my dad."

Yeah, that was her, she thought. Always thinking of her clients' shooting victims first.

"The least I can do is give you a ride back then," he offered. "No sense paying for a taxi if you don't have to."

Marnie knew she should decline, but the prospect of spending a little more time with Daniel won out. "Thanks," she said. "I appreciate it."

For perhaps the hundredth time in as many minutes, Daniel asked himself what the hell he thought he was doing. This time, though, he did it twice—one what-the-hell for driving Marnie back to her hotel, and another what-the-hell for insisting he follow her up to her room to make sure she arrived safely. A woman traveling alone couldn't be too careful, he'd told her. Even in small towns.

But he knew that was only part of the reason. In spite of having spent the last eight years trying to forget about her, he realized he was still powerfully attracted to Marnie Roberts. Maybe even more than he'd been in San Diego. He'd been a kid in San Diego, uncertain of himself and not especially confident where women were concerned. He'd always told himself that was why he'd fallen so hard for Marnie in the first place—because he'd been so inexperienced, and she'd seemed so sophisticated. But his experiences since then had only made him realize tonight just how special Marnie Roberts was, and how lucky he'd been to meet her when he did.

Not much had changed in that regard, he thought. She was still special. And he still felt lucky to have met her.

The dazzling, effervescent girl had blossomed into a stunning, elegant woman. As they'd chatted tonight, Daniel had been transfixed by her. By the changes in her. She seemed so much more confident, so much more poised than she had been before. Stronger. More seasoned. More womanly. She appealed to him in ways she hadn't before. Probably because he'd changed so much himself.

Now, as he stood behind her and watched her slip her key card into the lock of the hotel-room door, he didn't know what to say. What to do. How to act. He watched as the little green light flashed, followed by the click that said everything was okay. But nothing felt okay. And instead of signaling a go-ahead, the green light seemed to be a warning of some kind. Whether it was trying to warn Marnie or him, he couldn't have said.

The room was dark when she pushed the door open, and she mumbled something about having wished she'd turned a light on before she left.

"I'll get it," he volunteered. And before she had a chance to decline, he was pushing into the room past her, trying not to notice the soft swish and click of the door as it closed behind them, throwing them into darkness.

Well, not complete darkness, he realized, since the curtains were open and the scattered lights of Pepper Flats lay beyond—not as bountiful as they would be in a big city, but glittery enough to look as if someone had tossed a handful of diamonds onto a black velvet background. He and Marnie were, however, utterly alone.

And before he realized what he was doing, Daniel heard himself say, "Marnie, I'm sorry about the way things turned out in Del Mar."

She said nothing at first, only strode across the room and stared out the window beside him. Although he couldn't see her well in the darkness—he still hadn't switched on a light…but then, neither had she—he imagined her expression was probably much the same as it had been in the hospital waiting room. A little preoccupied, a little anxious, a little confused.

Finally, very softly, she said, "Are you?"

He expelled a long breath. "Yeah. I am. I shouldn't have left you that letter the way I did. I should have explained things to you face-to-face."

"Yes, you should have." She hesitated before adding, "Is that the only reason you're sorry?"

She wasn't going to make this easy, was she? Then again, he didn't deserve for her to make it easy. Hell, he'd brought this on himself by wading into the past in the first place, when he should have remained rooted in the present, where they had both seemed content to stay all evening. In spite of that, he added, "No. That's not the only reason. I also should have explained things better than I did."

Still staring out the window, she said quietly, "Oh, I think you explained pretty well. Your horses meant more to you than I did. End of story. It was good that you told me when you did, instead of leading me on."

"Marnie, that—" He halted abruptly, before he made things even worse. Was that what she'd thought after reading his letter? That she'd meant less to him than the animals he trained? Just the opposite had been true. That was why he'd had to leave the way he did— because Marnie was becoming so important to him, she was making him forget all the reasons he needed to succeed. But if that was the way she'd been feeling all this time, she wasn't going to change her mind just because he told her otherwise.

Ah, hell, he thought. Why had he even taken them down this road? Hoping to salvage what he could of the conversation, he said, "That week just didn't end up the way it was supposed to. I…"

Finally, she turned to look at him, but her face was still in shadow, telling him nothing of what she might be thinking or feeling. "You…what?" she asked, her voice completely void of emotion.

"I don't know," he said honestly. "What happened between us in San Diego… It just came out of nowhere. I was totally unprepared for it."

"I wasn't prepared for it, either, Daniel."

"I wasn't looking to get involved with anyone," he said.

"Neither was I."

"I was just starting out in my career."

"I hadn't even begun mine."

"And I just wasn't ready, that was all."

She was silent for a moment more, then repeated, quietly and carefully, "That was all?"

He knew it sounded lame, but he nodded anyway. "Yeah. I was just a kid eight years ago, Marnie. We both were. Can't I just say I'm sorry and let it go at that?"

She made a sound that was something between a humorless chuckle and a tsk of resignation. "You know, even without the apology, I *had* let it go, Daniel. Until I saw you tonight. And then, it was like I relived that whole week in ten seconds' time. But what was really strange was that, by the time we finished dinner, I'd almost forgotten about how it ended in San Diego. It felt like we were back there again, a few days before the end, and everything was fine."

Wow, she'd felt that, too? He'd experienced the same thing. That was why he'd offered to drive her back to her hotel, why he'd wanted to walk her to her room, why he'd apologized for what had happened, as if it were some minor transgression that could be excused with a heartfelt *I'm sorry.* And it was why—

Well. It was why he suddenly wanted to do a lot of things he knew he had no business doing. Which was all the more reason he couldn't do any of them.

"But we're not back there, are we?" she asked more softly. "And we can never go back there again. It's ridiculous to think otherwise."

She was right. He knew she was. But he wasn't ready to leave it behind just yet. She would probably only be in Hunter Valley for a little while. He might not see her again after tonight. So he turned to stare out the window again, thinking it might be easier to talk to her if he weren't looking at her. And he searched for the right words to say.

"You know, when you think about it, the two of us never really learned that much about each other that week. I knew you were rich and had just graduated from college and what you wanted to do with your future. But I didn't know much about your life's experiences—what made you the way you were."

She said nothing for a moment, as if she wasn't sure why he was saying what he was. Well, that made two of them.

Finally, she said softly, "No, I don't suppose you did."

He turned to look at her full on. "And you didn't know anything about mine, either."

She studied him in silence for another moment, then said, "No, I guess not. Just that you lost your mom when you were fourteen and went to live with your dad."

He nodded. "My mom and I were poor. I mean, really poor, Marnie. My dad never sent money he was supposed to send—because he didn't have it at that point—and my mom was almost never around because she had to work so much to keep us afloat. When she was around, she was too exhausted to do much more than make dinner, give me a hug and send me to bed. We did all our shopping at thrift stores, and we never had enough money to do fun stuff. We had to move around a lot, because she kept getting behind in the rent. It was a childhood full of insecurity and fear. And once I escaped it, I swore I would never go back. There was a time when I wouldn't have thought you could understand what that was like. But after what you told me about your father losing everything, I imagine it's not such a stretch, is it?"

She shook her head. "I understand the insecurity and fear," she said. "I understand the poverty. But I was an adult when all that happened to me. I was better equipped to understand the unfairness than a child would be. I'm sorry it was like that for you, Daniel."

He shrugged. "Yeah. Anyway, you need to know that about me for anything else to make sense. My experiences as a child are what define me as an adult. They're what drive me now, and they're what drove me in San Diego.

"Before I got to the Pacific Classic," he continued, "the only thing I could think about was winning. Because I knew that was my ticket out of the life I'd had up till that point. There were a lot of people—important people—who had their eye on me, ready to invest. I knew if Little Joe won the Classic, I'd have people standing in line to hire my services. And that was what I wanted most in the world back then, Marnie. To train champions."

"And you do," she said.

"Now I do," he agreed. "Back then, though…" He looked out the window again. "I wanted to make a big splash, be the guy everyone was talking about in Thoroughbred circles."

God, he'd been so young, Daniel thought now. So arrogant. To think that, at twenty-four, he could achieve the sort of success that a lot of trainers never saw in their lives. He'd thought he could take Little Joe to the Kentucky Derby and be one of the youngest trainers ever to win that race.

"Winning was the only thing that was important to me back then," he said. "That week I met you, it was to win the Classic. That was why I went to San Diego. Not to…"

Good God, he thought. He'd been about to say *Not to fall in love*. Where the hell had that come from? He'd been many things that week with Marnie—infatuated, preoccupied, distracted—but he hadn't been in love.

"Not to spend the week with a woman who was fun and vivacious and beautiful and—" He'd been about to finish with *and who made me forget about why I was really there*. He turned to look at her full on again. "I was there to win," he repeated. "That was my job. That was most important. When I failed, it meant starting all over again. And starting over required everything I had to give. There wouldn't have been anything left of me to give you, Marnie. The reason I left was all about me. It had nothing to do with you."

She studied his face in the darkness a moment, as if looking for the answer to a very important question. Finally, she asked, "And what's the most important thing to you now, Daniel?"

Her question puzzled him. Wasn't the answer obvious? "My job," he replied automatically. Hadn't he just told her that?

She nodded slowly. "Of course. That is, after all, what you do best. And you're the best person doing it."

Her comments puzzled him. She made it sound as though being good at what he did was a bad thing.

She bit her lip thoughtfully, her eyes fixed on his, glimmering in the scant moonlight that was filtering through the window. And damned if Daniel didn't find himself wanting to reach out to her, even after telling her—and himself—all the reasons he'd had to leave. She just looked so sad, and he couldn't stand it that he'd made her feel that way. Again.

Before he realized what he was doing, he lifted a hand to her face and cupped her jaw in his palm. "Oh, Marnie," he said softly. "I know it's too little too late, but I am sorry for the way things ended in San Diego. I was a dumb kid, and I behaved badly. And you deserved a lot better than that."

Without thinking, he dipped his head and touched his lips to hers. He had only intended for it to be a quick, chaste kiss. The kind two friends shared when greeting each other again after a long separation…or before saying goodbye one last time. He hadn't intended to lean forward again, after pulling back, to kiss her a second time. And he hadn't intended for that second kiss to be less quick and less chaste than the first. And then he was framing her face in both hands and kissing her a third time, his mouth slanted over hers as he teased the seam of her lips with his tongue.

Marnie covered his hands with hers and kissed him back, her mouth vying with his for possession. Just as it had in San Diego, their passion rose suddenly and burned hot. She tasted so sweet, and her body was so soft against his. He looped one arm around her waist and tangled the fingers of his other hand in her hair, gently tugging her head back so he could drag kisses along the line of her jaw and the tender column of her neck. She curved one hand over his shoulder and the other around his nape, kissing his cheek, his temple, his forehead.

Then their mouths met again, and Daniel just kissed her and kissed her and kissed her. She felt so good to hold, even better than she had before, and kissing her now was better than it had been, too. He couldn't help wondering what it would be like to make love to her again. He dropped his hand to her shoulder, then lowered it to her breast, his fingers curving into the soft flesh under her shirt. She gasped at his touch and tore her mouth from his, pulling her hands from his hair and face, taking a giant step backward.

"Stop," she said breathlessly. She took another step away from him and covered her mouth with the backs of her fingers. "We can't do this, Daniel. Not here. Not now. Not ever again. You just said your work is the most important thing to you, and I don't want to be put in the position of being second-best again." She swallowed hard, took another step backward. "We have to stop. Now."

She was right, he told himself as he tried to still his own ragged breathing. At least the part about them having to stop. The part about being second-best and his work being the most important thing…

No, she was right there, too, he told himself adamantly. As good as it might have felt tonight, being with Marnie again, his work had to come first. He was on his own and on his way, just as he'd always intended to be. And she'd started over without him, too.

"I'm sorry," he said. He chuckled mirthlessly. "Again."

"Daniel, I—"

He held up a hand to stop whatever she was going to say. "I should go," he told her. "It's a long drive back to my father's house."

She started to say something else, but evidently thought better of it. Daniel turned and started for the door, then halted. He couldn't just walk away and leave things as they were, unsettled. He'd done that eight years ago and regretted it.

"It *was* good to see you again, Marnie," he said softly. And since he was being honest, he added, "I hope we see each other again."

She didn't say anything, only stood silhouetted against the window, her arms wrapped around herself in a way that made him wonder whether she was doing it because she was cold, or because she just needed something—someone—to hold on to. In either case, Daniel understood. There was an emptiness clinging to him that he suspected would be there for a long time.

"Take care, Marnie," he told her.

Then he moved to the door, opened it and stepped through.

As he made his way to the stairwell, he couldn't help thinking he'd left Marnie the same way he had eight years ago. Without satisfaction or explanation. And with a lot of questions that neither of them would ever have adequate answers to.

Chapter Four

Louisa Fairchild didn't look much like the gentle, cookie-baking, apple-cheeked grandmother type that Marnie had been hoping she could make her out to be. On the contrary, there was an unmistakable air of haughtiness—even arrogance—about her. As Marnie followed her client and her client's attorney to a table at the back of a café across the street from the Pepper Flats police station—where Louisa had just undergone a second round of questioning—Marnie noted that the older woman carried herself like an Amazon.

She was tall and lean, handsome rather than beautiful, her skin tanned enough and her features weathered enough that Marnie sensed she preferred to be outdoors rather than inside. Her tidy chignon was the color of pewter, her eyes a deep, expressive blue, both features adding to the impression that Louisa was as strong and as durable as the fabled Australian outback. Dressed in a plain, long-sleeved blue dress and flat pumps that were probably intended to make her look both unobtrusive and harmless, she seemed neither. Her gait was a combination of elegance, economy and determination, the sort of stride that made it appear as if the ground she walked upon was higher than the rest of the world.

Then again, Marnie thought, the woman was a legend, and legends were always larger than life.

Robert D'Angelo, Louisa's attorney, pulled a chair from beneath the table for his client to be seated, then another for Marnie, then folded himself into a third. He was a nice-looking man in his late forties, his brown eyes hooded and shadowed by the remnants of restless or no sleep—not surprising, considering his client. His suit was an expensively tailored number that Marnie noted because the people she'd met in Australia so far had struck her as much more casual.

"Louisa, Louisa, Louisa," he began, shaking his head at his client benignly. He pronounced "Louisa" as "Louiser" with his broad Australian accent, his voice fluid and deep and lovely to listen to.

Marnie felt colorless in comparison, and wished she'd worn a brighter suit instead of the champagne-colored one she'd chosen. Then she remembered she didn't own any suits—or clothing—in vivid colors anymore.

Robert withdrew a pair of reading glasses from the

breast pocket of his jacket and perched them on the bridge of his nose, then reached into his leather brief-case for a file folder that was fat with papers. On its tab, Marnie saw Louisa's name, and she figured there was probably more included there than just information relating to her criminal charges. D'Angelo had been Louisa's attorney—or, rather, solicitor—for years.

Interesting that he would represent her in a criminal case, Marnie thought. Then again, maybe that wasn't so strange. She sensed Louisa Fairchild wasn't a woman who trusted others easily or made ready friends. Probably, Robert was one of the few people in her life with whom she shared both trust and friendship.

As if to illustrate that, he smiled at the other woman and said, "What are we going to do, my dear, about this spot of trouble you've landed yourself in this time?"

Sitting ramrod straight in her chair, Louisa met the solicitor's gaze unflinchingly. "I've not got myself into anything," she said. "It's Samuel Whittleson who's to blame for this mess. Him and his bad temper and his misguided notion that Lake Dingo belongs more to him than it does to me and that he has the right to say what happens to it."

Robert sighed the sort of sigh people gave when they'd been through something a million times and were resigned to having to go through it again. "Neither of you has a right to the lake right now, Louisa, not while your dispute is being reviewed by the court. So let's focus on this other matter instead." He looked at her over the top of his glasses in a way that made Marnie think about big birds of prey and their single-minded pursuit of lunch. "Now then. Just what the hell were you thinking to shoot Sam in the chest?"

Louisa leaned forward over the table, deliberately into Robert's space. The solicitor, not surprisingly, didn't back down an inch.

"We've already gone over this, Robert," she said.

The solicitor tilted his head in Marnie's direction. "For the sake of Ms. Roberts here, let's go over it again."

Louisa leaned back in her chair, expelled an irritated sound and threw Marnie a look that said she was not happy to see a representative from her PR team here in Pepper Flats.

Tough, Marnie thought. Clearly, Louisa didn't know how to conduct herself in a situation like this and needed help—something she'd employed a PR team for in the first place. Marnie would take care of the old woman, even if—or perhaps *because*—she wouldn't take care of herself.

"I was reacting," she said. Though, Marnie noticed, she was speaking to her attorney, not to Marnie. "Sam burst into my home in a fit of rage, completely uninvited."

"And the rage was due to?" Marnie asked. "I mean, if the feud has been going on for some time, what set Sam off on this particular day?"

Louisa glanced over at her. "How the bloody hell do I know? That man goes off for no reason. He used to be a pretty levelheaded bloke. I even liked him when he first bought the station next to mine. But the past few years, he's changed. He's got a hair trigger now, that one. And not just because we've been arguing over the lake."

"And how is it," Robert asked, "that you just happened to have such quick access to a gun? You were breaking the law, not having it locked up, which is another charge they're planning to press against you."

Louisa made a *pshaw* sound and waved an unconcerned hand at the solicitor. "Guns have to be cleaned, don't they?" she asked. "That's what I was doing when Sam barged into my house. I just hadn't unloaded it yet."

"How did he get in?" Marnie asked.

Louisa lifted her chin another notch. "I forgot to lock the door."

Marnie arched her brows skeptically. "That doesn't sound like the Louisa Fairchild that Division International represents, especially when she lives out in the middle of nowhere. And especially since the trouble over ownership of the lake began."

The other woman hesitated a moment before responding. "I forgot to lock it when I came back from Pepper Flats," she finally said. "I went into town for provisions and such, and I had my hands full coming in, so I guess I just closed the door and forgot to shoot the bolt."

"You forgot," Marnie repeated.

"Yes. I forgot." Louisa smiled with mock sweetness. "I'm an old woman, you know. Old women sometimes forget things like that."

"You may be eighty, Louisa," Robert said, "but I'd

wager you can still remember the color of the dress you were wearing your first day of school."

"Wasn't wearing a dress," she said. "My schooling came right to our station, over the radio. But I recall I was wearing my sister's hand-me-down dungarees that first time class was called to session over the wireless."

"My point exactly," Robert said, still grinning.

It was the first of many points made over numerous cups of weak diner coffee during the next half hour, and not very many of those points were dots that could be connected. On the surface, the story Louisa told seemed to make sense. She claimed the dispute over ownership of the lake had escalated gradually over the past year, from simple I say–you say bantering to an all-out legal assault. And once the solicitors had gotten involved, the gloves had come off. There had been episodes of vandalism she attributed to Sam—everything from the tire of her truck being deliberately flattened while she was in town to the windows of a deserted shed on the edge of her property being shot out—but she had no proof that he was responsible. And indeed, there had been similar episodes of petty mischief in this part of Hunter Valley that had nothing to do with Louisa or Sam and could very well have been the work of adolescents.

But Marnie could sense there was something the woman wasn't revealing, and Robert concluded the interview with Louisa looking no more pleased than Marnie was.

Clearly, Louisa wasn't going to make any of this easy.

Marnie wasn't quite able to hide her fatigue when she reminded Louisa, "The annual Fairchild Gala is just over a week away, and I know how important that event is to you."

Louisa nodded once, fiercely. "It raises hundreds of thousands of dollars so those children can receive equestrian therapy."

Children and horses were a cause near and dear to Marnie's heart. As a very young girl, she'd been a timid, anxious little thing who'd had difficulty making friends. But her mother had wanted to share her own love of horses with her daughter and enrolled Marnie in riding classes. At first, Marnie had been as intimidated by the horses as she was by people. But it hadn't been long before her fears evaporated and she came to feel confident instead. Ultimately, whenever she'd ridden, Marnie had felt powerful and graceful, and she'd come to love horses—especially Blue Boy. Riding instilled all kinds of wonderful feelings in children—strength, self-assurance, responsibility, love. And children with special needs, like the ones who received the proceeds from the Fairchild Gala, gained even more from the activity. The gala was for such a good cause, and it raised so much money.

For that reason more than any other, Marnie wanted to make sure it was a success. The only way to do that was to make sure Louisa's name was cleared, and people stopped thinking about her as a potential murderer. And the only way to do that was to present her as the victim in this situation, not the criminal. Of course, that was going to mean Marnie had to make the man Louisa had put in the hospital out to be something of an ogre....

She sighed fitfully and forged ahead. "If you want the gala to keep making that much money," she told Louisa, "then you're going to need to work with me on this. We have got to clear your name." She looked at Louisa intently. "We really should talk more this afternoon. About the ways you want Division to proceed with this, and how we're going to ensure the success of the gala."

Louisa eyed Marnie warily, as if she still wasn't sure why she'd hired a PR firm in the first place and wanted Marnie to go home. Then she said, "Why don't you come round to the house for tea? We can talk then."

Marnie nodded. "That would be lovely. Thank you, Ms. Fairchild."

"Miss," Louisa immediately corrected her. "I don't abide that *Ms.* nonsense. Either a woman is married or she isn't. There's no reason to blur the line."

Marnie's brows arched in surprise. She would have thought Louisa Fairchild would have been at the forefront of the women's movement when it started, but she didn't press the issue. "I beg your pardon," she said. "Miss Fairchild." She'd halfway hoped Louisa would extend the invitation to be addressed by her first name, but wasn't exactly surprised when no such offer was forthcoming. "What time should I arrive?"

"A bit before three, I reckon," Louisa said. "That'll give us plenty of time to chat."

With things tentatively settled—for the moment, anyway—Marnie and Robert collected their various files on Louisa and the three of them stood. Outside the café, Robert and Marnie traded cell numbers and made plans to talk again the following day, after she and Louisa had had a chance to strategize. Then Marnie shook hands with both Robert and Louisa, promising the latter she would arrive at her house by three. When she turned to leave, however, she stopped dead in her tracks. Standing across the street, in front of the Pepper Flats jail, his legs splayed wide and his hands settled on his hips in challenge, was Daniel Whittleson.

Daniel Whittleson, who had obviously just witnessed not only the friendly verbal exchange Marnie had shared with Louisa and her attorney, but the handshake, as well.

Daniel had come to the Pepper Flats jail to see if the detectives had made any progress on his father's case when he noticed movement on the other side of the street and turned in time to see Marnie talking to Louisa Fairchild and her attorney. At first, he'd thought he must be seeing things out of context, that Marnie was simply there by coincidence, not design. Then he'd watched her smile and shake hands with both of them.

So, naturally, he crossed the street and said, "What the hell is going on here?"

Louisa Fairchild opened her mouth to reply, but, not surprisingly, her attorney stepped in front of her and answered instead. "Louisa is conferring with her solicitor and a representative of a company in which she has interests. It's no concern of yours, Mr. Whittleson."

"The hell it isn't," he retorted. "Anything that woman does is a concern of mine. She tried to kill my father."

"We'll not discuss this any further," her attorney said. He turned to his client. "Louisa, I'll see that you get to your car safely." Then, erasing any doubt left in Daniel's mind that Marnie's presence in their company could still be a coincidence, the man turned to her and added, "Ms. Roberts, you and I can speak tomorrow after you and Louisa have had a chance to confer."

And then the woman who'd shot his father and the man who was going to try to have her found innocent of the crime strode off down the street, leaving Daniel and Marnie alone.

Daniel completed the steps necessary to bring them nearly nose to nose, telling himself it was because he was angry at her and wanted to violate her personal space, not because he hadn't been able to stop thinking about her all night and wanted to see if she smelled as sweet as she had when he'd held her the evening before.

Don't think about that now, he told himself. Don't think about that ever again.

"What the hell is going on?" he said again. And then it hit him. The work Marnie was in Hunter Valley to do was PR for Louisa Fairchild. "She's one of your clients, isn't she? You're here to make the woman who shot my father look good."

Marnie opened her mouth to reply, then closed it again and relied on a single nod as her response.

"We talked for almost two hours last night," he continued. "Didn't you think it might be important to let me know at some point that you came here to work for the woman who tried to kill my father?"

Marnie closed her eyes, as if steeling herself for something, then opened them again and met his gaze. "Daniel, I didn't mean to—"

"Didn't mean to what?" he demanded. "Didn't mean to lie through your teeth? Didn't mean to pump me for information about the crime so you could twist it around to suit your needs?"

"Oh, now wait just one minute," she told him, dropping her hands to her hips indignantly. "I didn't pump you for information. I was honestly concerned about Sam's welfare."

"Yeah, right."

"All I asked was how he was doing," she reminded him.

"And you asked what happened," he reminded her back.

"Because I wanted to make sure he was all right," she insisted.

He shook his head in disbelief. "You lied to me about why you're here."

"No, I didn't." But her tone was considerably less confident now. "I just wasn't exactly…"

"Honest?" he said. "Is that the word you're looking for?"

"Straightforward," she corrected him. But the correction was halfhearted at best. "Everything I've said to you is the truth," she added. He opened his mouth to argue again, but she pressed on. "Maybe I didn't tell you up front that I was working for Louisa, but I never said anything that was untrue. I *am* in Pepper Flats on business and I *did* read about Sam in the paper. And even if you don't believe me, the main reason I was at the hospital is because I *did* care about his condition. And I still do."

He settled his hands on his own hips in challenge. "I hear a *but* coming."

"But," she said with clear reluctance, "I also care about Louisa's condition. She may be a difficult woman, but she's not such a loose cannon that she'd shoot a man without provocation. There's more to what happened between her and your father than either of us knows. Maybe even more than the police know."

"She shot my father. That's all that matters," Daniel said evenly.

"Your father may have tried to assault her," Marnie shot back.

"That's ridiculous, and you know it."

"What I know," she said, clearly striving for patience, "is that I can't make any hasty judgments here. And neither should you."

"And what *I* know is that I can't trust a woman who's done her best to deceive me."

"Yeah, well, you should know about deception, shouldn't you?" Marnie retorted. "Since you clearly didn't mean a word of anything you said to me in San Diego that first time."

Daniel uttered an exasperated sound and drove a hand angrily through his hair. "This isn't the place for this," he said softly.

She nodded, a quick, brittle gesture. "No, it's not. But you know what? I think the two of us have said everything we need to say to each other, anyway. I think we each know where the other stands. There should be no reason to see each other again after this exchange."

Oh, Daniel didn't know about that. They hadn't even scratched the surface of all the things they needed to say to each other—not about the present or the past. Regardless of anything they might have said last night, it was clear that neither of them had put San Diego behind them. And, he was forced to admit, there were obviously still feelings between them. Those feelings might have changed from what they'd once been, but they were every bit as strong. Maybe even stronger. He told himself that everything associated with San Diego, including any leftover hurts or resentments, should stay in the past. It was bad enough they'd dredged up as much as they had. But somehow, he didn't think that was possible.

When Daniel said nothing further, Marnie lifted a hand to her forehead and closed her eyes, taking a deep breath to calm herself. Her voice was much more level when she began speaking again. "Okay, look. If I had really been trying to deceive you last night, I would have… I *wouldn't* have ended that…that kiss. And I would have…" She dropped her hand back to her side and opened her eyes, but she looked at something over his left shoulder. "And I would have done whatever I could to wheedle more information from you about your father or try to make you change his mind about pressing charges against Louisa." She looked straight at him now. "But you were the one who started things last night, Daniel, not me. I was the one to put a stop to them. So I'm the one who should be worrying about intentions and deception."

Okay, so she had a point.

"I admit," she added a little less vehemently, "that maybe I wasn't entirely straightforward with you last night—"

"Maybe you weren't entirely honest," he couldn't help interjecting.

She ignored him. "But I didn't press you for information about your father's case other than to ask how he was."

"You wanted to know what happened."

"Because I care about Sam."

"But you care more about your paycheck."

She glared at him. "Which is something you should understand."

The barb hit home. She was putting her career first, the same way he had in San Diego. The tables had been very effectively turned. Just as Daniel had done eight years ago, Marnie was sacrificing any chance the two of them might have for a relationship. Just as he had, she was choosing the professional over the personal. And, just as he had done to her, she was letting him know where he stood.

It was a place Daniel didn't much like standing.

When he was silent, she dropped her hands and said wearily, "I have to go."

"Yeah, you have to go make the woman who tried to kill my father look like an innocent lamb."

"No, I have to go do the job I was hired to do," she corrected him. "And that's to take care of a woman who can't—or won't—take care of herself."

And with that, Marnie turned and made her way around Daniel and up the street, leaving him alone to think about things he'd just as soon not think about.

And not just things related to his father's shooting, either.

Chapter Five

Marnie didn't make it to the end of the block before Daniel caught up with her. Any hope she might have entertained that he'd followed her because he wanted to apologize was dashed, however, when she saw the expression on his face. He looked angrier now than he had a few minutes ago, something she wouldn't have thought possible.

She still couldn't believe she had let him kiss her last night. And, even more unforgivable, she kissed him back. There had just been something about standing in the darkness with him, and hearing his soft voice saying he was sorry things had turned out the way they did....

But what difference did it make if he apologized? Eight years ago or today? She couldn't trust him. She'd be crazy to get involved with Daniel again, and his kissing her the way he did last night could certainly be construed as interest.

Then again, they'd both agreed it had been a mistake.

So why did she keep thinking about last night with such wistfulness and wishing it could happen again? Why did yearning pool in her belly every time she recalled the delicious caress of his open mouth along of her throat? Why was she still overcome by a shudder of heat at the memory of his hand closing oh-so-briefly over her breast? Why had she lain in bed last night wondering what it would have been like to have Daniel lying there beside her?

Pushing the unanswerable questions away, she said wearily, "What do you want now, Daniel?"

"I want to know what you're planning to do."

"Oh, really." She made the reply a statement, not a question.

"Yeah. Really. If you're doing PR for Louisa Fairchild, it means you're going to be working hard to make her come out of this thing looking good. Like she didn't try to commit murder."

"She *didn't* try to commit murder," Marnie countered. "She shot a man in self-defense."

Daniel uttered an angry sound. "You know that isn't true."

"And how do I know that?" Marnie demanded. "I only met your father once. Who knows what kind of person he is."

"You said he was nice to you."

"And that James Bond villain was totally devoted to his cat when he wasn't trying to blow up the world. Just because someone acts nice doesn't mean they're not capable of doing bad things. For all I know, your father has an arrest record a mile long."

"My father's never been arrested for anything. He did *not* assault Louisa Fairchild."

Marnie met his gaze levelly. "If memory serves," she said, "I recall you saying at one point in San Diego that you and your father weren't as close as most fathers and sons were, that you had a lot of…what did you call them? 'Father issues' when you were a boy."

His lips thinned into a tight line, and a muscle twitched in his jaw. "Don't bring my relationship with my father into this," he warned her quietly, his voice edged with barely restrained fury.

Marnie swallowed the guilt rising in her throat and said, just as quietly, "I'll use whatever information I have and do whatever I have to do to make sure I complete the job I was hired for."

She was trembling now with emotion. Oh, God, had she really just said the things she had about Daniel and his father? That was a horrible approach to take. She could perform the worst kind of character assassination against Sam in the media if she wanted to, and she could use Daniel's own admission from eight years ago as a springboard to do it. But that would be stooping to a new low. Then again, hadn't she just told him she'd do whatever she had to do to get the job done? For Marnie to make her client out to be the injured party, there was going to have to be another party that had done the injuring. And the only other person involved in the shooting was Sam. What other way was there to clear Louisa's name than to vilify Sam's? The worse Sam looked in this thing, the better off Louisa would be.

But could Marnie really do that? Jeopardize Sam's reputation, his career, and maybe even his legal case, just to make her client look better? Had she sunk that low?

Daniel went absolutely livid at her comment. Not that Marnie blamed him. But what was she supposed to say? What was she supposed to do? Her obligation was to Louisa, not Sam. And certainly not to Daniel.

Nevertheless, she backed down some—for now. "Look, all I know is what my client told me, because no one else has given me anything to go on. And my client says she shot your father in self-defense. From where I stand, that's totally credible, and that's what happened. So, yes, I'm going to be getting the word out that Louisa Fairchild was acting in self-defense when she shot an intruder in her home."

Daniel was clearly striving for calmness when he replied, "And when people find out that the person in her home was my father, they're going to think he's the criminal, not her."

Marnie gentled her voice some. "He shouldn't have been in her home, Daniel. She didn't invite him."

"Says you."

"Says she," Marnie corrected. "And unless she says otherwise, that's what I'm going with."

"You're going to make my father out to be the bad guy."

Very carefully, she told him, "I'm going to do my job." And because she couldn't quite help herself, she added, "You, above all people, should understand that."

For a moment, he only studied her in silence. Then, slowly, he nodded.

"So it's war then," he said.

She shook her head. "No. It's work."

"And that means more to you than common decency."

The smile she gave him in response was brittle. "What can I say? I had a good teacher."

He set his jaw hard at that, and his eyes went flinty.

Something cold and unpleasant knotted in Marnie's belly at the animosity that was burning up the air between them. Less than twenty-four hours ago, there had been a very different emotion in the air. But it had been every bit as passionate. So maybe that was it then, she thought. There had been passion between her and Daniel virtually from the moment they met eight years ago. It had exploded so brightly and burned so hot that week, it had nearly consumed them both. Within hours of seeing each other again, that passion had ignited once more. And now here it was, still burning, as bright and as hot as ever.

Except this time, it wasn't the passion of attraction. This time, it was the passion of aggression. It wasn't fueled by their fondness for each other; it was fueled by their bitterness. And somehow, she couldn't help thinking, that made it even stronger.

"This isn't over," Daniel told her. Then he turned his back on her and strode down the street.

Marnie turned and made her way in the opposite direction. She knew it wasn't over. That was the problem.

Fairchild Acres was very different than Marnie had imagined. The main house was a massive stone-and-stucco mansion with dozens of east-facing windows that must welcome the morning sun magnificently, and a quartet of arched entryways, any one of which could have been the main entrance. The place looked fairly new, however, not the sort of stately old manor she had been expecting. She knew the Fairchild family had lived in Hunter Valley for generations, but this clearly wasn't the house earlier members of the clan had called home.

As she'd driven across the two-hundred-acre property, Marnie had seen a number of outbuildings—barns and bungalows and storage facilities—along with paddocks and exercise areas for the horses. Fairchild Acres even claimed its own racetrack. And in spite of the owner's current legal problems, the place was alive with activity, adult horses running across the winter-brown fields, a handful of younger animals cavorting behind them. Exercisers and groomers saw to their equine charges, trucks made the rounds to deliver feed and other necessities.

Marnie had smiled when she'd seen a trio of kangaroos hopping across one section of now-barren pasture-land where horses would have been grazing in the summer months. Although much of Hunter Valley resembled parts of California, kangaroos weren't something she'd ever seen at home—at least not outside the San Diego Zoo.

Having grown up on a working horse farm herself—her parents had raised hunter-jumpers—Marnie knew a spread like this employed dozens of people in various roles, and Louisa doubtless had at least one or two members of live-in staff who worked in the main house. They were people whose jobs could be jeopardized if Fairchild Acres suffered financially because of the shooting. If the business went under, the horses would have to be sold and the property parceled out to whoever wanted a piece of it. More than a century of Fairchild sweat and care and love gone in no time flat, thanks to one rash act of one rash Fairchild. Marnie couldn't let that happen.

Just as she'd suspected, it wasn't Louisa who answered the door, but a graying woman in a uniform of sorts, a navy-blue skirt and white blouse, support hose and sensible shoes. She smiled benignly at Marnie and showed her to the library to wait for Louisa. As she followed the woman down a long foyer and past a sweeping staircase Marnie noticed that the house was decorated in a style very much like the estates she'd visited in San Diego, a sort of California casual with light breezy colors, simple but elegant carpets on teak floors and broad leaf patterns on the upholstered furniture. There were sketches of the estate grounds on the walls, and sleek, abstract sculptures dotted many of the tables. The overall feeling was…calm. Soothing. Serene. She couldn't imagine the house being the site of a shooting and suddenly wondered what room it had taken place in.

Thankfully, her brain didn't wander any further than that, because Louisa entered the library with her usual brusque greeting. She'd changed clothes and now wore khaki trousers and what appeared to be a hand-knitted sweater in varying shades of blue. Marnie had changed, too, before coming to the house, but had still stuck to the rules of business casual with charcoal trousers and a dove-gray cashmere sweater set.

Louisa moved to an overstuffed chair in a bay window on the far side of the room and sat down, then gestured to a chair on the other side of the window and invited Marnie to have a seat, too.

"You have a beautiful home," Marnie told her. "But it's not at all what I expected."

The old woman laughed. "You expected to see some crumbling old bit of stonework dating back to convict days, I imagine."

Marnie smiled. "Not at all. But I know the Fairchilds have called Hunter Valley home for some time, so I thought there would be a stately old manor with gables and turrets and maybe a widow's walk. This looks like something I'd see in Rancho Mirage back home."

"Well, it's true we Fairchilds have been here for a long time," Louisa said, "but the rest of the family weren't quite as business savvy as I am, and they never really made a go of the place the way they should've. I was the one who brought the place up right, and ten years ago, I rewarded myself with this house." She looked around the library. "I went to California a few times in my younger days. I always liked the people there—they seemed to live more slowly than the rest of your country. They have a lot in common with us Aussies in that respect. I reckon maybe I was trying to capture that feeling when I decorated. Didn't really do it consciously and never really thought about it till now."

"Well, it's lovely," Marnie said, then switched gears. "But down to business. The Fairchild Gala is just over a week away."

Louisa nodded.

Marnie opened her portfolio and withdrew a few pages she'd pulled from her file. "This is quite a guest list you have here," she said. "Weston Parnell and his daughter Darci, for instance." She glanced up at Louisa now. "He owns Warrego Downs in Sydney, doesn't he? That's one of Australia's premiere racetracks."

"Wouldn't be much of a gala without the Parnells," Louisa said crisply.

"No, I don't suppose it would," Marnie agreed. She looked at some other names. "Rex and Adeline Cambria of Cambria Estates Vineyards here in Hunter Valley. Tyler Preston of Lochlain Racing. His brother Shane.

Their parents, David and Sarah. Those are some of the most distinguished folks in Hunter Valley."

"Well, so am I," Louisa said indignantly. "You needn't make it sound as though I have trouble getting people to come to the gala. I invite guests from the four corners of New South Wales. And they've always made a point to come."

"Exactly," Marnie said. "Under normal circumstances, I know the party would go off without a hitch. But, Miss Fairchild, this year's circumstances aren't normal. You've shot a man." When Louisa opened her mouth to argue, Marnie pressed on before she had the chance. "Have you had anyone call to cancel since the shooting took place?"

Louisa shifted uncomfortably. "Some." With clear reluctance, she added, "And they've asked that their checks be returned."

Marnie nodded. "And it's not just going to be the party that will be affected, Miss Fairchild. Your business could suffer significant damage, as well. We have to get to work immediately to clear your name."

"And just how do you propose to do that?" Louisa asked.

Marnie braced herself. "First and foremost, you might want to consider dropping the charges you've brought against Sam Whittleson."

"What?" Louisa was outraged. "You must be joking. That man—"

"That man," Marnie interrupted, "might just consider dropping the charges he's going to press against you if you take the initiative to drop yours against him."

"Never," Louisa said, crossing her arms over her chest with a note of finality.

Marnie had been afraid that would be her answer. But she wasn't abandoning hope that she might be able to talk her client into that eventually. It was their best option in getting Sam—and the police—to reconsider. If the charges were dropped against Louisa, it would go a long way toward restoring her social and professional status.

For now, though, all Marnie could do was say, "At least give it some thought, will you?"

Louisa studied Marnie intently for a moment, then surprised her by saying, "I like you, Marnie Roberts. You call a spade a spade, and you don't back down when a crotchety old woman tries to cow you. I'm glad to know all that money I've sent to Division isn't being wasted."

Marnie bit back a smile, inordinately pleased to have won Louisa's acceptance. "Thank you, Miss Fairchild."

She grinned. Then she surprised Marnie even more by adding, "Call me Louisa. And why don't you check out of the Wallaroo Inn and move your things here to my place? You deserve a proper room, not some clapped-out water hole in Pepper Flats. Not to mention it will be one less charge for Division to put on my final bill."

As surprised as Marnie was at the invitation, she was grateful for it. "Thank you, Louisa. That would make our collaboration much easier."

That much settled, Louisa turned serious again. "Just how bad do you think this thing is going to get, with the press and the people of Hunter Valley and all?"

"You mean with gossip?"

Louisa tilted her head slightly. "Well, yes, that, too." Her words came out slowly and carefully, as if there was something else on her mind. "But what I really want to know is…" She sighed fitfully. "Well, just how deep do you think the press is going to dig into my background when they look into the shooting?"

Marnie eyed the other woman closely. "What are you afraid they're going to find out, Louisa?"

The older woman's eyes went wide at the question, but she quickly recovered. "I'm not afraid of anything."

But something in her voice suggested there might be at least one thing she was afraid of people finding out about her. What that might be, Marnie couldn't begin to guess. Louisa Fairchild didn't seem like a woman with secrets.

Very cautiously, Marnie asked, "You haven't shot someone else in the past, have you, Louisa?"

The older woman grinned. "Not that I haven't been tempted a time or two, but no. It's nothing like that. I just thought maybe, if it was a slow news day or something, people might be of a mind to go snooping a bit deeper than usual, and—"

"And what?" Marnie asked.

Louisa studied her in silence for a moment, then waved a hand airily in front of her face. "Oh, never you mind," she said. "There's nothing for either of us to worry about. I'm just being an old woman."

Marnie doubted that. Louisa might be eighty, but there was nothing old about her.

Before either of them could say any more, however, there was a rap on the library door. Both women turned toward it, Louise calling out, "It's open!"

Marnie first thought the man who entered must be an employee of Fairchild Acres. Then Louisa smiled at him, and it was clear he was more friend than employee.

She gave his hand a vigorous shake and patted him on the upper arm. "Shane Preston, what a pleasure."

One of the Australian Prestons, Marnie gathered. He was in his early thirties, she guessed, his hair the color of sand and sunshine and his eyes the dark blue of the deepest part of the ocean. He was handsome, tall and fit, and he carried himself with confidence. His smile came readily when he saw Louisa, and it was clear he liked her as well as she did him.

"Are you happy to see me because it's me, Miss Fairchild?" he asked. "Or because you know I've brought the wine for the gala?"

Louisa gave his arm an affectionate squeeze. "Both," she said. "Here, Shane, come meet someone. This is Marnie Roberts." She affected an air of self-importance as she added, "She's my PR woman from California."

Shane's sandy brows shot up at that, but his smile for Marnie was quick and charming. "All the way from

California?" he asked. As he extended his hand, he added, "What part?"

"San Diego," Marnie said as she shook his hand. His grip was firm in hers, which she appreciated. She hated it when men gave her a wimpy handshake because she was a woman.

"I may be heading your way in a month or two," he told her. "I'll be bringing some wines to the States for a tour."

"Look me up if you're in Southern California," she said. "I'll leave one of my cards with Louisa."

"Beauty," he told her. "I will."

"Shane's going to take Cambria Vineyards global," Louisa informed her. "Just you wait. Soon Cambria will be the label everyone's talking about."

"I hope you're right, Miss Fairchild," Shane said. "I hope you're right."

"But aren't you one of the Prestons of Lochlain Racing?" Marnie asked.

"Unfortunately," Louisa muttered, the pleasure that had been in her voice completely absent now. "He's the only one of that lot worth anything."

"Now, now, Miss Fairchild," Shane said with amusement, clearly having gone through this before. "If my family is good enough to invite to the gala, they're good enough to deserve your respect."

"All I respect is the money they give to my favorite charity. And that's the only reason they're on my guest list."

Shane shook his head, but he was still smiling. "One of my goals in life is to get you and my family on better terms. You've all got more in common than you realize." Before Louisa could respond to that, he turned back to Marnie. "Lochlain's actually more my brother Tyler's venture. I never had the same passion for racing and horses that he did."

"Shane's grandparents, Rex and Adeline—now they're good people—started Cambria years ago," Louisa said. "Then his aunt and uncle, Keaton and Cristina, took over. But they were killed in a terrible accident two years ago. Left their daughter Hilary in a wheelchair. With no one to run the business, Shane stepped in." She patted him on the back. "He's a good boy."

He actually blushed at the praise, Marnie noted. "Miss Fairchild..." he said. "You make me sound like a bloody do-gooder."

"Well, you are. And a good vintner, too," Louisa added. "I wouldn't have any wine but Cambria in my house."

He looked at Marnie and shook his head. "Sounds like she's trying to get work as *my* PR rep."

Louisa chuckled at that. "Thanks for bringing 'round the wine, Shane." She winked at Marnie then. "Let me know what I owe you for it."

"Same as always," he replied as he turned toward the door. "Not a cent. Save it for the gala. I left a check for the kids, too, from Cambria Vineyards. See you at the party."

"It was nice meeting you," Marnie said as he opened the door.

"And you, as well," he told her, lifting a hand in farewell.

After the door closed, Louisa turned to Marnie. "If I were fifty years younger…" She sighed dramatically. "Ah, well. So then, Miss Marnie Roberts," she continued, "I reckon we have a lot of talking to do. Like, for instance, you need to tell me all the nice things you're going to say to make me sound less like Jack the Ripper and more like Her Majesty the Queen. So let's get on with it."

Chapter Six

Marnie had just checked out of the Wallaroo Inn and was pulling her rolling garment bag behind her—bump, bump, bump down the hotel's front steps—when the wheel got caught on something and knocked the bag off-kilter. She turned in an effort to right it before it could fall, but spun around too quickly. As she struggled to right both herself and the bag, all she succeeded in doing was to lose her grip on it. That was when the bumping turned into one big thump as the bag went careening to the bottom of the stairs…right at Daniel Whittleson's feet.

She closed her eyes and groaned inwardly when she saw him standing there. Either she had the absolute worst luck of any woman in the world, or he was stalking her. And considering the way they'd parted that afternoon, she was betting on the former. He'd been so angry, she'd figured he never wanted to see her again.

As if reading her mind, he greeted her with a stiff, "No, I'm not stalking you. I'm tired of driving back and forth between my father's house and the hospital twice a day, so I've decided to take a room here in town."

She hesitated before replying, trying to decide the level of her own anger as she framed her response. Finally, she decided on a cautious, "There are other hotels besides this one."

He nodded. "Yeah, I know."

Which meant he had almost certainly chosen the Wallaroo Inn because he knew Marnie was staying there. He probably wanted to keep an eye on her. What was that saying? Keep your friends close, but your enemies closer? He didn't consider her a friend anymore. Not that they'd really been friends to begin with. Anyway, it didn't matter now, because she was checking out.

To his credit, Daniel bent down and righted her bag, collapsed the handle back into its pocket and picked it up. "Where do you want this?" he asked, his voice a shade less hostile than it had been the last time she saw him.

She made her way warily down the rest of the steps and stopped in front of him. "My rental car," she told him. "But I can take it from here." Grudgingly, she added, "Thanks for halting its progress before it rolled into the street."

"Yeah, halting it with my shin," he said pointedly.

She felt her face flame at that. Was he goading her? Trying to pick a fight? Or did he just feel as awkward around her as she did around him?

"I'm sorry," she told him. "It's not like I did it on purpose."

He arched a dark brow that made her wonder if he believed her…and also made heat seep into her midsection, because there was just the merest hint of sexual suggestion behind the gesture. He'd done that in San Diego, too. Looked at her with that single arched brow whenever he was feeling amorous. Evidently, she was no less immune to it now than she'd been then.

How could she still find him so attractive after some of the words they'd exchanged—and such a short time ago, at that? Passion, she reminded herself. It was that weird, mixed-up passion that walked a thin line between love and hate. You had to be cruel to be kind. And all those other old song lyrics that had never made any sense until now.

Ignoring the sensation in her stomach as much as she could, Marnie reached for the suitcase, closing her fingers over the handle Daniel still gripped. As soon as her hand brushed his, the heat in her belly bloomed, spiraling outward until it threatened to overwhelm her. Automatically, she snatched her hand back, hoping he didn't notice her strange reaction. But when she braved a glance up at him, she saw his cheeks stained with pink and his pupils gone wide and his lips parted in surprise. And she knew that he'd felt it, too, that same jolt of awareness that had rocked her.

"I'll…let me…" he stammered. He dipped his head down toward her suitcase and tried again. "I mean, I can carry it to your car for you. It's pretty heavy."

She willed him to make some dumb joke about packing bricks in there. Something to lighten the mood, even if it was lame. Instead, he said something that only threatened to increase the tension between them.

"Is it too much to hope that you're checking out because you're going back to San Diego?"

Just like that, the vast coil of heat unwinding inside her chilled. "You'd like that, wouldn't you?" she said, her voice as cool as the rest of her. "But I don't run away just because the stakes get higher."

He closed his eyes at that, his head tipping backward a little, as if she'd slapped him. "I guess I deserved that."

Not really, she thought. What he deserved—what they both did—was an uncomplicated environment in which to meet again, so they could address whatever might still be lingering between them in a way that didn't invite verbal barbs. Marnie had never been the sort of person to go for the jugular. No matter how angry she became with someone, she was generally able to remain calm and collected. She might be outraged, but she never let her negative feelings show. Something else that made her good at her job was her ability to negotiate, and do it with tact. With Daniel, however…

"Louisa has invited me to stay at her house," she told him. "It will make it easier for the two of us to confer."

"Confer," he repeated blandly. "That's one of those PR words for 'conspire,' isn't it?"

Marnie lifted a hand to her temple and rubbed at the headache that seemed to come out of nowhere. "Yeah. Yeah, that's it. Louisa and I can't wait to get together and start plotting our takeover of New South Wales." She dropped her hand and looked straight at him. "Here's another PR word for you. 'Whittleson.' It's the one we use instead of 'paranoid.'"

He started to retort then snapped his mouth shut. She noticed his grip on her suitcase tightened, and she half expected him to hurl it out into the street. Instead, very softly, very evenly, he said, "Look, can we try to talk about this like two adults?"

"I don't know. Can we?"

Well, evidently not, she thought. Because her response had been kind of childish.

He must have thought so, too, because he shook his head and muttered, "Never mind. Tell me where your car is, and I'll stow this for you and be on my way."

Marnie pointed to the blue sedan parked at the curb a few cars down from where they stood. As he turned to walk in that direction, she said, in a more adult tone this time, "Daniel."

He turned around again, his face a silent question mark, and suddenly, Marnie couldn't remember what she had been about to say. Something apologetic, maybe. Something that might at least let them come to a tentative truce. But she stopped herself, because she remembered she had a problem with trust. Except now it wasn't just a problem with Daniel. Right now, she didn't much trust herself, either.

She really didn't know him, she reminded herself. One week eight years ago hardly counted, even if the two of them had been so physically intimate with each other. Oh, they'd talked about their pasts…a little. And they'd shared their dreams for the future…to a point. And they'd revealed one or two secrets about themselves…that really weren't all that secret or revealing.

Just how well had she known Daniel Whittleson in San Diego? How well did she know him now? For that matter, considering the way she'd responded to him since meeting him again, how well did she know herself these days?

A big part of PR was the ability to study people and read their minds and anticipate both their thoughts and their behavior. Usually, Marnie was pretty good at that. With Daniel she was hopelessly lost. She had no idea what was going on in his head. And she had no clue how to anticipate his behavior. For all she knew, the reason he wanted to talk like adults was to uncover her plans for Louisa and then sabotage them before Marnie had a chance to put them in place. Not that she blamed him for that. But neither did she trust him.

What was worse, she honestly feared he might very well be able to do that before she could stop him. He had the same effect on her now that he'd had on her eight years ago. The moment she came within twenty feet of him, everything in the world disappeared but him.

"Never mind," she finally told him.

He hesitated a moment, then turned toward her car again. Marnie followed, maintaining a slight distance from him. When she thumbed the car's key fob to pop the trunk, Daniel pulled it open the rest of the way and dropped the suitcase inside.

"So you'll be at Louisa's," he said after slamming the trunk closed again.

She nodded.

"Then maybe I won't check in to the Wallaroo Inn, after all."

"Why not?"

He lifted a shoulder and let it drop. "My dad's place is next door to Louisa's—not as close as they'd be in the suburbs, but not that far apart. And how does that old saying go? Keep your friends close but your enemies closer?"

Something in Marnie's chest tightened at hearing him utter the very thing she'd been thinking herself not long ago. How about that? she thought. For the first time since meeting up again in Australia, they were finally on the same page.

As Daniel sat beside his father's bed watching the old man sleep, he did his best to focus on the steady rise and fall of Sam's chest as he inhaled and exhaled, and to think about nothing but his father's hopefully speedy recovery. But no matter how hard he tried, he couldn't quite banish the memory of that sizzle of…something…

Something yearning and incandescent…that had arced between him and Marnie when her hand had landed on the suitcase handle beside his.

How could he still want her after all this time? Especially after some of the words they'd exchanged since meeting again, and the knowledge of what she could potentially do to Sam and his reputation. He supposed there was no way to explain sexual chemistry. There were just some people destined to be attracted to each other, even knowing they wouldn't be good together. Eight years ago, he hadn't been able to resist Marnie. He'd been a kid blindsided by an unexpected passion and had reacted without thinking. And although he'd been blindsided by her again, now he was a grown man in better control of his feelings. There might still be sizzling chemistry between them, but he could keep himself in line now where she was concerned.

Right, a voice inside him piped up. The way you kept yourself in line at her hotel.

He pushed that thought away, too. Now that he *was* on his guard around her, what had happened last night would not happen again.

His father began to stir in his bed, and Daniel sat forward, hoping this time his dad would do more than open his eyes and mutter a few sentences before surrendering to sleep again. Mostly all Sam had been able to do was recognize his son, express his gratitude for Daniel's presence, curse Louisa Fairchild and then tumble back into slumber. It looked, for a moment, as if he were going to repeat that cycle, but this time, after cursing Louisa, Sam slowly lifted a hand and placed it over his son's.

And then, in a voice as rough as sandpaper, he said, "I want to go home, son. When are the docs going to let me do that?"

Daniel smiled in a way that he hoped was reassuring. "I'm not sure, Dad. They said less than a week. But it's only been three days."

The passage of time seemed to shock Sam. His brown eyes widened, and he lifted his other hand to smooth it over the dark hair that was even more liberally threaded with silver than the last time Daniel had seen him. "Only three days?" he asked. "Crikey, I feel like I've been here three months." He met his son's gaze fiercely. "You've got to get me out of here, Danny. I've got a farm to run. I can't get anything done if I'm lollygagging in bed."

Daniel smiled again, genuinely this time. His father was sounding more like himself. Daniel had seen that things were running reasonably well on the farm in Sam's absence. Still, he wouldn't return to the States himself until his father was on his feet again.

"Yeah, well, you were shot in the chest," he reminded his father. "You need to do some lollygagging in bed if you want to recover from something like that."

"Bah. Lucky shot. That crazy old woman couldn't hit the side of a barn most days."

Daniel knew that wasn't true. Louisa Fairchild had

grown up around guns and had learned to hunt at an age when a lot of kids were still struggling with table manners. Sam was the one who'd been lucky—that she hadn't hit any major organs or, worse, killed him.

Which, Daniel thought reluctantly, said something for the self-defense angle. If Louisa had wanted to kill his father, she would have put a bullet straight through his heart. The fact that she'd missed anything major indicated she hadn't been aiming when she pulled the trigger—and might have been struggling.

No way, he immediately countered himself. Maybe she hadn't been aiming, but she hadn't been struggling, either. Not with his father.

Sam was two decades younger and a good foot taller than Louisa Fairchild, and when he wasn't confined to a hospital bed with a bandage wrapped around his chest, he was strong enough to fight men nearly twice his size. And usually win. The thought that he might have tried to attack Louisa was… Well, it was unthinkable.

Even so, Daniel asked, tentatively, "Dad, what were you doing in Louisa's house?"

Sam's bushy eyebrows arrowed downward, and he frowned. "I just wanted to talk to her. I thought maybe if she and I could chat about the lake without our solicitors, we'd have a better chance of coming to terms."

That wasn't what his father had said the last time Daniel spoke to him. During that phone conversation, Sam had said he never wanted to trade words with that cantankerous old woman again, that from now on, he was going to let the lawyers handle everything.

"Why did you go in without knocking?" Daniel asked.

"I did knock," Sam told him. "But she didn't answer. I knew she was in there, though, because the door was ajar. So I went inside."

"You shouldn't have gone in without her permission," Daniel said, surprised by his father's admission. That was so unlike his dad.

"I just wanted to talk to her," his father said again. "And I was being completely reasonable. But Louisa didn't see it that way. We were in the library, and she went to the gun locker, took out a revolver and told me to get out."

Daniel wondered if the sedatives were messing with his father's memory, or if Louisa was lying about the gun. Very carefully, he said, "In the police report Louisa claimed she already had her gun out and was cleaning it when you stopped by."

Sam's expression grew thoughtful, as if he were trying to remember. Then he nodded slowly. "That's right," he corrected himself. "The gun was on a table. But it didn't look like she was cleaning it. It looked like she just had it out."

Like maybe she was fearful about something? Daniel wondered. Or someone?

"I was being completely reasonable," Sam said again. "But Louisa can't be when it comes to that damned lake. We began to argue, and then she went batty, and she picked up the gun and shot me."

It couldn't have been that simple, Daniel thought. He hadn't spoken to Louisa Fairchild for some time, but from what he'd heard, the woman still had all her faculties. Arguments sometimes escalated to dangerous levels, but neither Louisa nor Sam was the type to act rashly. Not unless something else was going on.

Daniel lifted a hand to his eyes and rubbed them wearily. Maybe it would be better if he and his father talked about something else. Sam had always liked hearing about what was happening at Quest, so Daniel switched gears and caught the old man up on what was going on stateside, and how excited everyone at Quest was to have a horse poised to win the Triple Crown in barely a week's time.

"And little Melanie sitting astride Leopold's Legacy when he wins it," Sam said with a cackle of laughter. "She must be giving the jockeys a lot to grumble about, being so female, snaking that title right out from under the lot of them. She's a firecracker, that one. She'll go far. And how are Thomas and Jenna?"

"Fine," Daniel said. "In fact, they're headed this way in a couple of days for the Galena Silver at Rosehill. Should be interesting, since they'll have a horse running against one from Lochlain Racing. Thomas and David Preston are still at it after all these years, competing to see whose farm, and whose horses, and whose business are superior. Even if David has stepped down and moved to Sydney with Sarah, Tyler's picked up the competition in his father's wake and run with it."

"Bah," Sam spat. "Tyler Preston couldn't come close to filling David's shoes. He'll never be half the man his father is."

Daniel winced and wished he'd never mentioned Tyler Preston's name. There were still a lot of hard feelings between the two men over a decision in a recent race in which they'd both had horses entered—the Queensland Stakes. It was a decision that had gone against Sam and favored Tyler and was still, at least as far as Sam was concerned, in dispute. Daniel, for his part, had tried to stay out of it as much as he could, though he was naturally more inclined toward his father's side of the story. Still, Tyler was a Preston, and even if the Australian Prestons and the Kentuckian Prestons weren't always on the best of terms, Daniel felt a certain amount of loyalty to the family.

The one undisputed fact was that Sam's horse, More Than All That, which had crossed the finish line at the Queensland Stakes by a country mile over Tyler's entry, Lightning Chaser, had been discovered after the race to be full of steroids that had enhanced his performance— illegally. Sam insisted he knew nothing about it—and Daniel believed him. His father was a horseman to the bone and would never do anything that might jeopardize the health of anyone's animals, never mind his own. Daniel was confident that whoever had injected the horse had had some other kind of stake in the race—a bet, most likely—and had administered the drug himself or hired someone at the track to take care of it.

Of course, Sam had accused Tyler Preston of being the one to drug his horse, for the very reason that More Than All That was the only animal who stood a chance of beating Lightning Chaser. Daniel, however, wouldn't go that far. Tyler was as dedicated to the care and well-being of his animals as Sam was. But Sam's accusation had done nothing but fan the already-climbing flames.

Interesting, Daniel thought now, rather uncomfortably. His father seemed to be making a lot of enemies in Hunter Valley. Louisa Fairchild. Tyler Preston. Both of them people Sam had gotten along with reasonably well before, even when differences of opinion had come up. What was going on that Sam didn't seem able to mend fences the way he once had? He'd never been the kind to nurse grudges, even when he'd been right and the other party wrong. He'd always been able to compromise or, at the very least, see the other side with some degree of fairness.

Daniel told himself he was being silly. There was nothing wrong with his father. For God's sake, Louisa had shot him. And Tyler had accused Sam of cheating and harming an animal, both of which were pretty much unforgivable sins in Sam's book.

"I need to rest now, son," Sam said suddenly, closing his eyes. "Damned meds are making me sleepy again."

"No problem," Daniel told his father. "I'll be here if you need me."

Sam shook his head slowly. "Don't lie about here," he said, his voice weak now. "I've got all these nurses to take care of me. Go do something fun."

"What makes you think this isn't fun?" Daniel asked.

His father smiled thinly. "Go," he said. "Take the afternoon for yourself. I'll still be here when you get back."

Over the next few days, Marnie did her best not to think about Daniel or Sam but focus on Louisa—the client upon whom her job depended. But even though she pulled out every PR trick in her book to spin her client's image in a more positive light, guests of the gala who had RSVPed in the positive were still finding reasons why they couldn't attend—or supply a check. And the RSVPs still unaccounted for were barely trickling in. The party, mere days away now, was on the verge of being canceled completely, and talk in Hunter Valley about the shooting was still rampant, little of it favoring Louisa.

And then there was Daniel.

Every time Marnie had seen him, he made her feel more confused and uncertain. She still cared for him, she admitted Monday as she sat in Louisa's library again, looking over a story about her client in that day's paper. Even after everything he'd done and said—both in San Diego and here—there was still a part of her that yearned to sit down with him and sort it all out.

The fact that she could feel that way after so much time and amid so many conflicting emotions told her that whatever had passed between the two of them eight years ago wasn't just a superficial affair. If it had been, they would have both let it go a long time ago. They wouldn't have responded to each other the way they had in Marnie's hotel room that first night. And there wouldn't still be sparks flying between them every time they encountered each other.

Don't think about it, she told herself as the memory of his mouth on hers erupted in her brain again. Think about Louisa and the gala and the fact a lot of kids are going to miss out on some much-needed services—not to mention you might lose your job—if you don't hurry up and make things right.

There was no way she could sit down and sort things out with Daniel anyway. Not while the two of them were on opposite sides of a criminal case. And, anyway, Daniel had offered no indication that he wanted to work things out with her. He didn't even want to sort things out with Sam and Louisa.

As if conjured by the thought, Louisa entered the library, and Marnie looked up from the newspaper. Louisa must have been working outside with the horses, because she wore a woolen jacket, now unbuttoned, over a bulky sweater and corduroy trousers that had seen better days. She snatched a wide-brimmed canvas hat from her head as she crossed the room, running a hand over her steely hair.

"Louisa, we got two more RSVPs for the gala today," Marnie told her without preamble, "both declining. It isn't looking good for this year's event, I'm afraid."

Louisa's expression didn't change, but something in her eyes dimmed a little. "Well, it'll be their loss, won't it?"

"No," Marnie said. "It'll be the children's loss when the charity doesn't get its usual check from you. And it will be your loss, too, because this is doing nothing to restore your status in the community." Louisa opened her mouth to object, but Marnie hurried on. "Look, have you given any more thought to dropping the charges against Sam Whittleson?"

Marnie braced herself for a negative reply, since she'd already broached the subject with Louisa several times to no avail.

"I will not drop the charges against that old codger," Louisa said levelly. "He assaulted me."

Marnie waffled over whether or not to ask the next question, then figured she had nothing to lose. "Are you so sure about that?"

Louisa gaped at her. "You think I'm lying about Sam Whittleson assaulting me?"

Marnie shook her head. "I'm just asking if maybe there's a possibility that the word *assault* is a little strong for what really happened. Just what did Sam do to you, Louisa? You never have said exactly, other than he barged into your house and attacked you. Did nothing happen to precipitate the attack?"

Louisa jerked up her chin and stared down at Marnie with an expression that could have turned fire to ice. "He lunged at me," she finally said.

"Lunged," Marnie repeated.

Louisa nodded.

"Lunging doesn't necessarily equate with assaulting."

"It does in my book."

Marnie eyed her more intently. "Why did Sam lunge at you?"

"Because we were arguing."

"At what point, exactly, did Sam lunge at you?"

The other woman hesitated before finally admitting, "It might have been when I picked up the gun."

Marnie chose her words carefully. "You know, Louisa, there's a chance that Sam might have seen your picking up the gun as a threatening action. He might have thought you intended to shoot him. It might have been *him* acting in self-defense. At least to his way of thinking."

Louisa gasped, clearly insulted. But she said nothing.

So Marnie ventured further, "Why did you pick up the gun?"

"To make a point," Louisa said.

"And that point was?"

"That I was mad as hell."

"Louisa, you have to drop the charges against Sam," Marnie urged her gently. When the other woman opened her mouth to argue again, Marnie held up a hand to stop her. "He didn't assault you. He didn't attack you."

"He was trespassing."

"Okay, maybe he was trespassing," Marnie relented. "But if you drop all the charges against him, there's a good chance we can talk him into dropping all the charges against you. And those charges are considerably more serious than the ones against him. You shot a man, Louisa," she added soberly. "Even if it was an accident, had things gone differently, he might have been killed. You need to stop for a minute and think about that."

Louisa opened her mouth again, then shut it. Finally, she looked down at her weathered hands spread open on the table. Hands that had held a gun and fired it at another human being. Hands that might have taken a life, had things turned out differently.

Then she looked up at Marnie again. "All right," she said. "If you can get Sam Whittleson to drop the charges against me, then I can probably see my way clear to dropping the charges against him."

Slowly, Marnie released the breath she hadn't been aware of holding. "Thank you, Louisa. I'll go see Sam tonight."

It would take police involvement to dismiss those charges, but if Sam made clear in his account of the events that the shooting had been accidental and occurred after he tried to take the gun from Louisa, the police would have a much more accurate account on which to base their decision on whether or not charges were warranted.

Of course, seeing Sam tonight would mean seeing Daniel, too, since Sam had been released from the hospital into the care of his son. There was no way Daniel was going to let Sam see Marnie without being present for the conversation himself. So it wasn't just Sam Whittleson Marnie was going to have to win over, it was Daniel, too. And somehow, Marnie suspected the younger Whittleson would prove to be the more difficult of the two.

* * *

Daniel was in the office of Whittleson Stud going through some paperwork when he noticed something strange about his father's finances. He'd thought he would do his old man a favor by paying some of the bills that had been sitting neglected since the shooting so Sam wouldn't have to worry about them, but noticed that the balance in the station's operating checkbook was dangerously low. Thinking his father must have intended to make a deposit just prior to the shooting, Daniel had looked at the registers for the other accounts, including his father's personal checking and savings accounts, and had found their balances to be much lower than they should have been, too.

He made a mental note to ask Sam about it when he was in better shape, before Daniel returned to the States. In the meantime, he went ahead and paid the bills that were about to come due and left the others for later. Then he went to the kitchen and poured himself a second after-dinner coffee to enjoy out on the veranda. It was a beautiful night, crisp and cold, with thousands of stars scattered across the sky and no moon in sight.

He had just folded himself into one of the creaky rattan chairs on the veranda when a pair of headlights came bouncing up the long drive to his father's house. Probably a neighbor coming to call. Sam had just been released from the hospital that day, and Daniel had been fielding calls all afternoon from people wanting to know how he was doing. Thankfully, he was doing well—

even better than the doctor had anticipated—but it was going to be a few more days at least before he was able to handle the day-to-day running of the farm. Daniel had arranged for a nurse to come to the house every day for as long as was necessary, something that would lessen his worry once he was back in Kentucky.

Well, lessen his worry about his father's physical health anyway. There was still that potential character assassination that Marnie could be starting any minute. But every time he tried to rouse indignation and resentment over her actions, he was instead beset by memories of that kiss in her hotel room. Or their easy camaraderie over dinner that first night and how quickly they'd fallen back into comfortable companionship before he found out she was representing Louisa.

Dammit, why couldn't he bring himself to hate her? Why did the good things about Marnie so outweigh the bad?

He watched the car coming up the drive until it halted at the foot of the walkway that curved up to the porch steps and its lights went dark. Whoever was inside took a moment to gather his things together, then pushed the door open and—

No, not *his* things, Daniel immediately corrected himself. *Her* things. The driver of the car was a woman. A woman whose dark auburn curls he'd know anywhere. Even the intermittent light of the car's interior couldn't diminish the loveliness of the slender leg that emerged from the car as the door was pushed wider. The cool evening breeze tangled in her hair as the rest of her appeared, framing her face with auburn fire. Something squeezed his heart when she closed the car door and the light was gone, taking the image of her with it. Then that something let go again when the bottom stair creaked beneath her step, because the soft sound told him she was close.

Well, that and her intoxicating fragrance, which the breeze carried over to him when it finished its dance with her hair.

She didn't come any higher than that first step, though, as if she weren't sure what her reception would be. Instead, she halted half in and half out of an irregular rectangle of light that spilled from the living-room window over the stairs and down to the walkway. She wore a straight denim skirt under a white T-shirt and short denim jacket with rhinestone buttons, each glittering with a different color in the pale light.

Something about those buttons reminded him of the Marnie he'd known in San Diego. She was so serious now, but something of the old Marnie always got through. At the hospital, it had been the ribbons and beads of her jewelry. Now it was rhinestone buttons. She might not be the effervescent girl he used to know, but she wasn't quite the cool sophisticate she presented to the outside world, either.

"Hi," she said softly. "I wondered if maybe you and I could talk. Without arguing this time, I mean."

"That's a pretty tall request," he said, only half kidding. "What do you want to talk about?"

She hesitated a moment, then, even more softly than before, said, "About Sam and Louisa and the possibility of *both* of them dropping charges. I've talked to Louisa, and she gave me some information about the incident that the police haven't shared with us, Daniel. It's information she may not have given them the first time out."

"Which could land her in a lot of trouble," Daniel pointed out. "Cops don't look too favorably on people who withhold information in a shooting."

She took another step up. "Look, let's just forget about the police for a minute, okay? Let me just tell you what Louisa told me."

"All right."

"She said she never intended to shoot your father, that she pointed the gun at him because he was making her angry and she wanted him to calm down."

"Threatening someone with a gun is supposed to calm them down?" he asked dubiously.

"We don't know how heated that argument got, Daniel. Louisa was scared, and she reacted instinctively. Your father did, too, by grabbing for the gun. They were both struggling with it when it went off. Louisa shouldn't have pointed the gun at Sam, but he shouldn't have been in her house in the first place. And they both had their hands on the gun when it fired. They are equally at fault for what happened. Either they can both press charges and go to jail, or they can both drop the charges and stay out of jail."

Daniel said nothing, mostly because he didn't know what to say. It was true that his father shouldn't have been in Louisa's home if she hadn't invited him there. It was also true that his father had been as unforthcoming with information as Louisa had. Maybe that was because both of them felt responsible for what had happened.

Maybe.

"Look, I just want to talk to Sam," Marnie said. "You can be there, too. I want to tell him Louisa's version and see how he reacts, or if he adds anything to the story that he didn't tell the police. Then you and I can go talk to the detectives and ask them to drop the charges."

He thought about that for a moment, then nodded. "Okay, you can speak with my dad. As long as I'm there, too."

"Of course. Thank you."

She started to step up onto the porch, but hesitated when Daniel rose. "I'm not making any promises, Marnie."

She smiled sadly. "I know you're not," she said quietly. "You never do."

That was where she was wrong, he thought. Maybe he hadn't made any promises to Marnie in San Diego, but he'd made one to himself after that. He'd promised himself he would never let himself get so lost in his emotions again that he forgot about what was most important—training horses to win races. He'd kept that promise for nearly a decade, too.

"I just want to talk to him, Daniel," she said again.

He took a step backward, clearing the way to the front door. "He's upstairs watching TV. I'll ask him if he'll see you."

Chapter Seven

It wasn't easy, but over the course of the evening, Marnie was able to draw Sam out enough that he admitted the shooting went much the way Louisa had described, and she convinced him to go over these new details again with the police and encourage them to drop the charges. As the two of them talked, Sam had begun to remember parts of the incident he'd been fuzzy on before. Or, at least, had claimed not to remember. Marnie honestly wasn't sure if the man's recollection of the shooting was genuinely vague or if there was something he was trying to hide.

But at least with both parties agreeing to this version of the shooting, Louisa was less likely to be viewed as someone intent on murder. And Sam would save face, too. He had felt threatened and reacted the way anyone might have with a gun pointed at him. Marnie would simply spin the shooting as a terrible accident that could have happened to anyone.

Nevertheless, there was still much work to do if she wanted to save the gala. She had to confer with the police as early as possible tomorrow morning to ensure the charges against both Sam and Louisa were dropped, and then get the information out to every media outlet she could find. Time was of the essence now. The gala was only a few days away. And there was still no guarantee that she could get people to change their minds about coming. If only there were something else she could do, but what?

Those were her thoughts as Daniel walked her to the front door. He'd been uncharacteristically quiet all evening, and had let her do most of the talking.

"Thank you for letting me see your dad," she said as he opened the front door to let her out.

"Thank you for getting Louisa to drop the charges against him," Daniel replied. "Though I have to admit, I'm not sure how I feel about this new version of the events. I still can't imagine my father lunging at an old woman, even if she was holding a gun on him."

"It sounds like he and Louisa both have let this Lake Dingo dispute escalate to the point where they're both behaving out of character."

"Still," Daniel said, shaking his head thoughtfully, "I think there's something else going on with my dad that's stressing him out way more than usual."

"What else could be going on with him?" Marnie asked curiously.

Something in Daniel's expression told her he hadn't meant to voice his concern. He shook his head again, more deliberately this time. "Nothing," he told her a little too quickly. "I'm sure it's nothing."

She was going to ask more, then reminded herself she had completed the job she'd come to do. Whatever else was going on with Sam Whittleson was Daniel's concern, not hers. So why did she find herself wanting to tell him that if he needed to talk, she was there for him? That whatever he was facing with his father, she wanted to help him get through it. But what was the point? For one thing, he would never ask for help from a woman who'd spent the last week threatening to cast his father in a less-than-stellar light. For another thing, even if he did, Marnie wouldn't be around to help him. Once the gala was over, she'd be finished with her work here and returning to San Diego. She had other jobs to do, other clients to take care of. After this week, there was little chance she would see Daniel Whittleson again.

The realization should have filled her with relief. Instead, she was overcome by an almost overwhelming sense of melancholy.

"I guess I should get going," she told him. "It's late."

He nodded. "Yeah, and I have to get up early tomorrow."

She braved a smile. "The day starts early on a horse farm."

"Actually, tomorrow I'm driving into Sydney to see the Prestons. So I have to get up even earlier if I want to get all the morning chores done first."

Marnie frowned. "But the Prestons live here in Hunter Valley."

He shook his head. "No, not the Australian Prestons. The Kentuckian Prestons. Jenna and Thomas came to Sydney for the Galena Silver at Rosehill that ran yesterday. They're leaving in a few days, and I want to see them before they go back. I'm having lunch with them tomorrow."

Marnie nodded and was about to say good-night to Daniel, when something clicked in her brain and made her hesitate. The Prestons were world-renowned horse-people. Even better, they were well respected. If Marnie could get Tom and Jenna Preston to come to the Fairchild Gala on Friday, chances were good that a lot of the people who had canceled might change their minds and suddenly become available that night. And Marnie would bet good money that the RSVPs that hadn't come in yet would suddenly arrive with an abundance of acceptances.

That was it, she thought. That was how she would save the Fairchild Gala—and Louisa Fairchild, too. If Tom and Jenna Preston attended the event, it would be tantamount to giving their stamp of approval to Louisa Fairchild and go a long way toward bringing her back into the Hunter Valley fold. And when Sam Whittleson dropped the charges against her, Louisa's reputation and standing in the community would be fully restored. Just as important, Marnie thought, Louisa's contributions to the children's charity would not be compromised.

But it didn't sound as if the Prestons were going to be in Sydney long. She would have to work fast—and try hard—to make them come to the gala. Of course, if she could get Daniel to help plead her case, that might go a long way toward convincing them.

"Daniel," she said, knowing he had little reason to help her out at this point, but hopeful that he would just the same, "I know you and I haven't been on the best footing lately, but can I ask you a huge favor?"

He looked understandably surprised but all he said was, "What?"

He'd probably be outraged by the idea after everything that had happened since she'd come to Hunter Valley, but she had an ace up her sleeve that might ensure his help. It was an ace she'd told herself she would never be reduced to using, but she was desperate.

"Help me convince the Kentuckian Prestons to come to the Fairchild Gala on Friday."

She hadn't been wrong about his response. "Why would I help you get my employers to attend a party thrown by the woman who tried to kill my father?" he asked pointedly.

"For one thing," Marnie said, "Louisa didn't try to kill your father. It was an accident. They've both said so."

He said nothing, but studied her mulishly, clearly still not willing to help.

"For another," Marnie continued, "the gala benefits

an excellent cause, and this year's party isn't going to
be able to contribute near the usual amount, thanks to
everyone breaking rank around Louisa. That charity has
come to depend on the money raised by the gala, and
without it, the children are going to lose out on a lot of
needed services."

Daniel still wasn't going for it, so out came the ace
from Marnie's sleeve.

"Besides," she said frankly, "you owe me after what
you did in San Diego."

She really didn't want to present herself as a victim, and
she didn't want him to think she was still smarting over
what had happened eight years ago. But she had been a
victim of sorts, and, truth be told, she *was* still smarting.
If looking pitiful and playing on any lingering guilt Daniel
might have about his behavior in San Diego meant
securing thousands of dollars for a worthy cause, Marnie
wasn't going to lose any sleep over playing the card.

The tactic clearly hit home, but it was obvious Daniel
was in no way happy about it. "All right," he said reluctantly. "I'll do my best to help you get the Prestons to
come to the gala. But they're planning on going home at
week's end because they don't want to miss the Belmont
Stakes on Saturday, so it's not my fault if they decline."

Damn. Marnie had forgotten about the Belmont
Stakes. Of course they would want to see their daughter
ride in that race.

"But there may be one reason they'd stay," Daniel
said softly.

Hope flickered in Marnie. "What is it?"

"Just let me do the talking tomorrow when we see the Prestons," he told her.

"We?" she asked warily.

He nodded. "Yeah, we. You can drive into Sydney with me, and we'll both talk to them."

Marnie wasn't sure she wanted to be cooped up in a car with Daniel for four hours—two there, and two back. "How about I meet you there? I have some other business in Sydney, and I'm not sure when I'll be ready to come back."

She didn't know if he believed her or not—and she'd just told him another lie, because she had no business in Sydney. But he nodded and said, "Okay. Meet me in the lobby of the Four Seasons at noon. We can go up to Tom and Jenna's room together."

"Thank you, Daniel. I appreciate it."

"But, Marnie," he said as she turned toward the front door.

She hesitated, looking back at him again. "Yes?"

"After this, you and I are even. With this thing between Louisa and my dad, and…" He scraped a hand nervously over the back of his neck and sighed deeply. "And with San Diego, too."

As if her feelings about that week could ever be resolved, she thought. Nevertheless, she nodded. "It's a deal."

And without another word, she turned and walked out of Sam's house. The entire time she made her way down the steps and walkway to her car, she felt Daniel's eyes on her back. Sure enough, after she was inside the car and started the engine, she looked up at the front door and saw his dark figure silhouetted there. He had one arm propped on the doorjamb, his forehead leaning against it. Even from this distance, he looked weary and drained and hopeless. Much the way Marnie felt herself.

No, not hopeless, she told herself as she threw the car into Reverse. Hope*ful*. At least about the Kentuckian Prestons. If they agreed to come to the gala, all would be well. And if they didn't...

Well, she wouldn't think about that now. The same way she wouldn't think about a lot of things. Like the way Daniel had looked at her just as she was about to say good-night, as if he wasn't sure what he should do or say next. It was the same way he'd looked at her that first night in San Diego, when he'd walked her to her front door. As if he'd wanted to kiss her, but wasn't sure he should. Marnie had taken the initiative then and kissed him.

She was sure he hadn't been thinking about that tonight, of course. No, he'd probably been wondering if he should even be polite to her. But his expression had been much as it had back in San Diego. And Marnie's reaction had been the same, too. She'd wanted to take the initiative and kiss him. In spite of everything that had happened eight years ago in San Diego. In spite of everything that had happened this week in Hunter Valley. In spite of the fact that there was no future for them after tomorrow...

But she didn't want to think about that, either.

* * *

Marnie stood beside Daniel as he knocked at the door of the Prestons' suite at the Sydney Four Seasons Hotel, inhaling a few slow breaths in the hope that it might steady her breathing a little. She told herself she shouldn't be nervous. She was on a roll, after all. She'd called Robert D'Angelo, Louisa's attorney, a half hour ago, and he'd told her that after the police spoke again to Louisa and Sam, it would only be a formality before all charges were dropped and the case closed. Marnie would get the word out to the proper media outlets later today, hopefully along with the news that Tom and Jenna Preston would be attending the Fairchild Gala.

Now all Marnie had to do was deliver the invitation—engraved, no less—that she'd brought with her. And not leave until the Prestons agreed to come. At this point, she was desperate enough to do just about anything to get them to accept.

She was giving her sweater one last nervous tug when the Prestons' door was opened by a smiling woman with laughing eyes who immediately made Marnie feel at ease. She'd spent much of last night trawling the Internet to learn everything she could about Jenna Preston and her husband. Marnie knew Jenna was fifty-five years old, had four children and two grandchildren, and she and Thomas had been married for nearly forty years. They called Quest Stables in Woodford County, Kentucky, home, but traveled extensively throughout the world for both business and pleasure. When Marnie looked past Jenna into the hotel room, she saw Thomas Preston, but he had his back to them and his cell phone pressed to his ear, deep in conversation.

Jenna was dressed in a simple but stylish green dress that would have been bland had she not accessorized it with a chunky necklace, bracelet and earrings of oversize, colorful beads. She was smaller than Marnie had expected, no more than her own five-four, and had auburn hair, too. But where Marnie's hair was an unruly tangle of curls when she didn't take pains to tame it, Jenna's hair had soft waves that seemed to caress her face. The older woman was pleased to see Daniel standing there, but obviously puzzled by Marnie's presence.

"Hey, Daniel," she greeted him. "Tom and I are almost ready. Come on in."

"I hope you don't mind," he said, "but I brought along a…friend…for lunch."

Whoa, whoa, whoa, Marnie wanted to say. *Lunch?* He wanted her to join them for *lunch?* That was even worse than being cooped up in a car with him. With other people around, she was going to have to pretend that she and Daniel were actually comfortable together.

Then an even more confusing realization crowded into her brain. *Friend?* He was introducing her as a *friend?* To Jenna Preston? That was the way you introduced someone when you were embarking on a new romantic relationship and didn't know what else to say. Jenna might infer that the two of them were an item.

Now Marnie would really have to pretend she and Daniel were comfortable together.

The way Jenna smiled at Daniel's comment, it was obvious that was exactly the way she'd interpreted the term *friend*. "Of course we don't mind," she said, apparently delighted Daniel had brought a date. "The more, the merrier. It's about time you brought along a *friend* for something."

Oh, great, Marnie thought Jenna sounded as though she was already mentally reviewing potential sites for a wedding reception.

But there was little Marnie could do about it now. To decline at this point would not only look strange but would also prevent her from extending the invitation to the gala. So she smiled her way through introductions as best she could and made the proper small talk as the four of them made their way down to the lobby restaurant for lunch.

When they were all seated and had placed their orders, Daniel turned to Jenna. "Actually, Jenna, there's an ulterior motive for Marnie's being here at lunch with us."

Marnie told herself not to be nervous, that all she was doing was inviting the Prestons to a party. Just because her job was on the line, and hundreds of kids might miss out on opportunities to make their lives better, that was no reason for her to feel nervous, right?

Yeah, sure.

Jenna looked from Daniel to Marnie curiously, then back at Daniel. "Really?" she said with a smile. "Silly me. I assumed you were bringing her because she's beautiful and charming and lovely to talk to."

Marnie made herself laugh and hoped she didn't sound as anxious and uncomfortable as she felt.

"Well, that, too," Daniel said, *almost* sounding sincere. "But there's another reason."

Jenna looked curiously at Marnie, who launched into her spiel. She explained that she worked for Louisa Fairchild and told Jenna and Thomas about the annual Fairchild Gala. She said that when Louisa Fairchild discovered the American Prestons were going to be in Sydney, she wanted to be sure they received an invitation, which Marnie then withdrew from her purse and handed to Jenna. As Jenna opened the envelope and scanned the engraved script on the heavy card, Marnie sang the praises of the charity that had come to rely on the money raised every year, and described the benefits the children received from equestrian therapy.

As she spoke, Jenna set the invitation on the table in front of her instead of sharing it with her husband, something that told Marnie the woman had made up her mind to decline right away.

Sure enough, as Marnie's speech wound down, Jenna said, "Please extend our thanks to Mrs. Fairchild—"

"Miss," Marnie corrected her automatically. "Miss Fairchild."

"Miss Fairchild," Jenna amended. "Please extend our thanks, but my husband and I will be catching a flight home the day of the party, so we won't be able to attend."

There was a coolness in her voice that indicated that even if she and Thomas hadn't been leaving that day, they still wouldn't come. Probably for the very reason Daniel had stated last night. Why would they attend a party given by the woman accused of shooting the father of one of their employees? And Daniel obviously wasn't just an employee, either. He was clearly a good friend.

As if realizing what Marnie had been thinking, that his friendship with the Prestons was affecting their reason for not attending, Daniel told Jenna, "It looks like the charges against Louisa Fairchild are going to be dropped, and that she's no longer going to have charges pressed against my father."

If Jenna was surprised by the news or the change of subject, she didn't let on. "Really?" she said.

Daniel nodded. "My father's much clearer on the details now, and it would appear that the shooting was an accident."

"I see," Jenna said. "I suppose, all things considered, that's good news, isn't it?"

"It's just good to have the facts and know what really happened," Daniel told her.

She nodded.

"It's too bad you won't be able to attend the gala," Daniel added. "Your nephew Shane was one of the first to accept."

Jenna looked interested in that. "Shane's attending?"

This time Daniel was the one to nod. "Yep. Tyler will

be going, too. And your brother-in-law David and his wife, Sarah, are going to drive to Hunter Valley from Sydney."

Marnie felt Daniel's knee nudge hers under the table and she almost started. Then she realized he wasn't being flirtatious. He was trying to cue her. As to what, exactly, she wasn't sure. But she did her best to follow up.

"The Australian Prestons are always a fixture at the gala," she told Jenna. "If you were going, maybe you could have made the drive to Hunter Valley together."

Instead of Jenna, it was Daniel who said, "Oh, I don't know, Marnie. The Kentuckian Prestons and the Australian Prestons don't always get along too well."

"Oh." Marnie didn't have to feign her surprise. "I see." But when she looked at Jenna again, the other woman actually appeared more interested in the party now than she had been a few minutes ago.

"That feud is old news," she said, waving a hand airily.

"Is it?" Daniel asked.

"Of course," Jenna said. "Isn't it, Tom?"

Thomas Preston was much taller than Marnie had expected. He easily topped six feet and was very handsome, with brown hair and dark blue eyes. Marnie couldn't help thinking that the Preston children must all be good-looking.

"Well, actually, Jenna—"

Before he could finish, Jenna looked back at Marnie. "David and Sarah are really coming?" she asked. "And the boys?"

Marnie nodded. "As I said, they were the first to

RSVP." And they hadn't canceled, so she hoped that meant they still intended to come.

Jenna smiled. "Then we'll absolutely be there. Won't we, Tom?" she added, turning to her husband again.

"But the Belmont Stakes—" Thomas started to object.

Jenna cut him off again. "We can leave right after the party on Friday. We'll charter a private jet. New York is about fifteen hours behind Sydney, so we'll be getting there well before the Belmont Stakes run."

"We'll be exhausted," Thomas told her.

"No, we won't," she assured him. "We can sleep on the plane." Jenna turned back to Marnie and smiled. "My husband and his brother David have always had a bit of a rivalry going on between them, you see. The American Prestons versus the Australian Prestons, you might say. My children—Andrew, Brent, Melanie and Robbie—have continued it with their cousins Tyler and Shane. Even though, as I said, it's old news, David and Sarah have avoided us the whole time we've been here."

"So then, there is a feud," Marnie said, confused.

"No, there's a rivalry." Marnie's confusion must have shown, because Jenna added, "Our family tree isn't terribly blighted. It's just a little…thirsty," she finished with a smile. "Thirsty for the water of relationship. Families shouldn't compete, should they? They should all get along. Maybe we'll have another chance at this gala."

Jenna pulled the invitation toward her. "Please thank

Miss Fairchild for the invitation. And tell her the American Prestons will be there with bells on."

"Wonderful," Marnie said. "Louisa will be delighted."

Chapter Eight

*D*elighted didn't begin to cover Louisa's feelings by the night of the gala, Marnie thought as she watched from the mezzanine above the ballroom as her hostess—and client—made her way through the crowd below. Once the shooting had been ruled accidental and news had gone out that the American Prestons were coming to the gala, a significant number of people who had previously declined suddenly found room on their busy social calendars to attend, and any outstanding RSVPs came in with their *Yes, I will be able to attend* boxes checked.

Now the Fairchild estate was packed to the gills with anyone who was anybody in Hunter Valley—and in Sydney, Newcastle, Wollongong and a handful of other cities to boot—all arrayed in their finest, most glittery attire. From her vantage point on the mezzanine that wrapped around the small ballroom, Marnie could identify a handful of people. She recognized Jenna and Thomas Preston, of course, who were virtually surrounded by admirers, and not far from them, Thomas's brother David and his wife, Sarah, were talking with a different group. Marnie grinned. Every time she saw Jenna and Thomas, they'd somehow managed to work their way closer to David and Sarah. She felt confident that before the night was out, whatever tension there was between the two families would be resolved.

There must have been two hundred people down there, she thought, and scores of others were wandering through the house. Louisa had left the first floor open for guests. White-jacketed servers threaded their way through the partygoers with trays of champagne, and open bars had been set up at opposite corners of the ballroom. A long buffet of finger foods spanned one wall, and other servers made their way discreetly through the room offering more.

Marnie herself twirled a flute of champagne in one hand, but she'd barely tasted the bubbly. She'd had to drive into Sydney to find an appropriate dress for the affair, since she hadn't actually planned on attending until Louisa insisted she should enjoy the fruits of her labors and unwind after a job well-done. Still, the simple black gown with spaghetti straps was conservative enough that Marnie could look professional, and the faux-pearl choker and earrings added an air of sophistication she rather liked. She'd swept her hair up as well as she could in two Art Deco–styled combs, but errant curls still tumbled free about her neck and face. She told herself they gave her an air of indifference, like some fabulous forties film star, and pretended it was supposed to be that way.

"You look nice."

She turned quickly at the deep voice that murmured low near her ear, a voice she hadn't heard for days—and one she'd feared she would never hear again. Something warm and wonderful fluttered in her belly, then she was flooded by heat when she turned to look at him. Daniel was so handsome, dressed in a classic tuxedo à la Cary Grant and sporting his own slender glass of champagne. His appearance reflected her golden age of cinema fantasy, and she smiled at the realization.

He smiled back, but quizzically. "What's so funny?"

She shook her head. "Nothing. I'm just surprised to see you here, all things considered."

He shrugged. "The charges have been dropped, and the shooting's been classified as an accident."

"Your father and Louisa are still on opposite sides of a legal dispute," Marnie reminded him. "The rights to Lake Dingo."

He shrugged. "That's between the two of them." He sounded tired of the whole thing. "All I know is that my father and I received an invitation to this thing, for some reason—"

The reason to invite the two men had been part of

Marnie's PR campaign. It hadn't had anything at all to do with her hope that at least one of them might actually come.

"—and since Dad couldn't make it," Daniel continued without missing a beat, "I figured the least I could do was come and eat enough of Louisa's food and drink enough of her champagne for two people."

"How is Sam?" Marnie asked.

"He's doing fine." Wryly, he added, "He's sorry he couldn't come to the party. He's recovering from a gunshot wound."

Marnie had the decency to wince.

Daniel leaned forward and braced his elbows on the mezzanine banister, closing both hands around his glass. "I'm sorry. I shouldn't be sniping at you."

His comment surprised her. "Why not? I'm the person who had the charges dismissed against the woman who shot your father."

He looked at her. "You're also the person who got the charges against my father dropped. I figure it evens out."

Marnie leaned her hip against the railing and eyed him thoughtfully. "Sounds like someone's been doing a little thinking the past few days." She nodded toward the champagne in his hand. "Or else a lot of drinking tonight."

He studied the glass as if he were looking for the answer to some very important question in its contents. "I've been carrying this glass around since I got here," he told her. "I'm not really much for champagne."

She nodded. "Then it must be the thinking that's

brought about this change of…" She'd started to say heart, then thought better of it. "Mind," she finished instead.

"I haven't really changed my mind," he told her. "Or heart, either," he added. "I'm not completely happy with the way things turned out. I still have to come to grips with the idea that my father could go after an old woman, even one who pulled a gun on him. But I am glad the charges against him have been dropped. He needs to move forward now. And I think he is. He even mentioned something today about maybe taking a vacation when he's up to it." He smiled. "A safari in Africa."

"Africa?" Marnie echoed. "That is ambitious."

Daniel nodded. "Yeah, maybe the shooting was a wake-up call for him. He and Louisa have to see that they've let the lake dispute get too far out of hand and they need to step back and let their lawyers do their jobs."

"I agree."

Marnie looked down at the crowd again and easily found Louisa, dressed in a long-sleeved, tomato-red dress with cuffs and hems trimmed in marabou. Two dyed red ostrich feathers fluttered from the gray hair piled loosely atop her head. Marnie wouldn't have thought Louisa had it in her to be such a showgirl. She wondered with a smile what other secrets the old woman was harboring.

"I know Louisa and Sam will never be friends," Daniel said thoughtfully, his gaze following Marnie's. "But at least maybe they can coexist with some degree of harmony. Regardless of what happens with the lake."

"Surely the courts will take both their petitions into consideration and try to reach a compromise."

Daniel nodded. "I'm actually going to talk to both attorneys about getting a moderator involved. I figure it can't hurt, and maybe an impartial third party will be able to look at the situation with a fairer eye. If Dad and Louisa could get that settled, it would be one less thing for me to worry about where he's concerned."

Daniel was looking down at the crowd with a distracted expression similar to the one he'd worn that night at his father's house while she was talking to Sam. Marnie was about to ask what else was worrying him, then realized he must have been referring to his father's health. "But the doctors said Sam is going to be fine, didn't they?"

He glanced up at the question, but didn't answer right off, and still had that faraway look in his eyes. Finally, he said, "What? Oh, right. Yeah, he's going to be fine. He's making his way around the house pretty well, and made his own meals today. And there's a nurse coming in every day to be with him until the doctor gives him a clean bill of health. He really doesn't need me around anymore."

"Then what else do you have to worry about?" Marnie asked.

Again, he paused before replying, but this time the hesitation was more deliberate. "Nothing," he told her. "There's nothing. Just…"

"What?"

He shook his head. "Nothing. Just a son worrying too much about his aging parent, that's all."

Marnie smiled. "Sam's only…what? Sixty?"

"Sixty-one."

"I don't think it's time to look into nursing homes just yet, Daniel."

Something in his expression indicated he wasn't so sure about that, but all he did was tilt his head toward the crowd and ask, "What kind of bird do you think Louisa killed to get those feathers?"

Marnie laughed at that. "I don't know. One that's indigenous to Las Vegas, I'm guessing."

Daniel straightened to his full height, a full head taller than Marnie. As he gazed down at her with his dark eyes, his expression was even more intent, and the easiness she'd begun to feel with him evaporated, replaced by the edginess she'd felt that first night in the hospital.

She might have been successful in putting Louisa Fairchild and Sam Whittleson on the same page, but she and Daniel were still separated by a chasm a mile wide. Even if Marnie wasn't working for Louisa, there was no future for the two of them. His work still meant more to him than anything. She'd thought in San Diego that he was the kind of man who could make deep personal commitments that lasted a lifetime. But, clearly, he was a textbook case commitmentphobe. She couldn't let herself feel anything for him but the wistful and melancholy affection one might feel for an old flame. And even that was being generous, considering the way he'd hurt her.

She wasn't going to put herself in a position where that might happen again. Not that he was offering…

"I gotta hand it to Louisa," he said. "She knows how to live. This house is three times the size of my father's. It isn't every day you go to a party at someone's house and find yourself in their ballroom."

"Don't Jenna and Thomas have a house this big?"

"Oh, sure. But they brought up four kids in it and still share it with the family. Louisa has this all to herself." He was thoughtful a moment. "Interesting that she never married and started a family. It's unusual for a woman of her generation to stay single."

"Oh, I don't know," Marnie said. "She's a very strong woman. And strong women of her time often flew in the face of society. Having spent a week with her, I can see she prefers her own company." She looked down at the crowd again. "There are times when I can totally understand that. This party is an absolute crush. I wish it wasn't so cold outside. It would be nice to take a walk and get some fresh air."

"Good idea," Daniel said.

"It's like forty degrees out there," Marnie reminded him.

"Who says we have to go outside? The whole first floor is open to guests. Though you've probably seen the entire house by now."

"Actually, I've seen very little of it," Marnie told him. "I've spent all my time either in my room or working in the library. I've been trying to stay on top of my other clients back home, but there's only so much damage control you can do online. There's a certain prince, for instance, who wants my head on a platter alongside his prison-issue beans and rice."

Daniel's expression turned quizzical. "Come again?"

Marnie shook her head. "Never mind. You don't want to know the details. Suffice it to say, if you ever find yourself in a compromising position with a mambo dancer, check to see if she has maracas under her skirt."

"Okay, that confuses me even more."

"Never mind," she said again, grinning. "You promised me a tour of the house. At least, what's open for the party."

"So I did."

When he extended his elbow, Marnie was sure he was only doing it to be polite, but she still hesitated before taking it. Then she thought, Oh, what the hell. She had a flight home booked on Sunday. Tomorrow would be her last full day in Australia. She might as well enjoy what little time she had left. Especially since she would likely never see Daniel again. At least the two of them would be parting on better terms this time than they had in San Diego.

Not that the thought brought her much comfort.

They dodged a few other couples who had found their way to the mezzanine as they headed back to the entrance. At the bottom of the stairs, they were greeted by one of the white-jacketed waiters, who took their glasses. The farther away from the ballroom they went, the fewer people they saw. At the very back of the house, they found themselves alone in a spacious solarium, probably because of its distance from the party. Marnie couldn't even hear the music from the ballroom anymore.

Despite the room's emptiness, there were a few lamps burning, indicating it wasn't off-limits to guests. On the far side of the entry were floor-to-ceiling windows that looked out onto what Marnie knew was an expansive and well-manicured backyard that spilled into woods—it was the view from the guest bedroom she was occupying. At night, however, those windows looked out onto darkness. The solarium was filled with plants, many of them leafy tropical trees in excess of eight or ten feet, interspersed with furniture of an equally tropical feel, bent rattan with fat flowered cushions. Marnie's and Daniel's footsteps echoed on the marble floor, then went silent as they stepped onto one of many thick oriental rugs.

"It's like Queen Victoria goes to visit the colonies," Marnie remarked. Indeed, it was a room fit for a queen and had the feel of old empire about it. "I bet Louisa spends a lot of time in here. It's nice, isn't it?"

Daniel shrugged. "It's okay, I guess. A little too much, if you know what I mean."

It occurred to Marnie then that she'd never seen anyplace Daniel called home. He'd visited her condo once or twice during the week he'd been in San Diego, but he'd been staying at a hotel when he was there. She couldn't remember him ever mentioning his home eight years ago. He'd said he lived in Kentucky now and worked for Quest. But he hadn't said anything about the actual place he called home.

"So then I guess you don't have a cozy little mansion waiting for you back home in Kentucky, huh?" she asked.

He laughed at that. "Ah, no. I actually live at Quest."

She was in no way surprised by the discovery. To Daniel, work and home were one and the same.

"Tom and Jenna have several cabins for their senior employees and guests," he explained, "and I live in one of those. It's nothing fancy, but it suits my needs."

"Mmm," she said noncommittally. Sounded as though Daniel didn't have too many needs these days. Then again, had he ever?

"So what is Quest closer to, Louisville or Lexington?" she asked.

"Lexington. We're in Woodford County."

We, Marnie noted. He'd said *we,* as if they were all one big happy family at Quest. But that didn't surprise her, either. A man who was married to his work would consider his coworkers family and his workplace home. Marnie couldn't imagine what that must be like. As much as she enjoyed her work at Division International—recalcitrant princes and gun-toting octogenarians aside—she couldn't see herself ever thinking of her job as a part of her personal life. At the close of business every day, she left her work at the office and went home. A real home, with lots of creature comforts and things that spoke of who she was—which was a lot more than a PR person for Division International.

Unfortunately, her work life was way busier than her personal life, meaning that at the end of the business day, she often didn't have a lot to do. So that kind of sucked.

"Well, *I* think the room is lovely," she told Daniel now as she turned around to look at him.

He said nothing for a moment, only studied her in silence. Then, very softly, he said, "You're lovely, too."

Something hot and frantic ignited in Marnie's midsection. His voice was low and level and potent, and when she saw the way his eyes darkened when he looked at her, the heat and turbulence only increased. Then he took a few steps toward her, and her insides exploded, all white and blinding incandescence.

As he drew nearer, he said, even more softly, "So I guess with the charges dropped against your client, and with her party being such a success, the business you came to town for is pretty much finished."

Marnie nodded. As much as she hated to admit it, there was no reason for her to stay in Hunter Valley any longer.

"Which means you'll be going home soon," Daniel added, closing the distance between them even more.

She nodded again. "Day after tomorrow, in fact."

He halted in his tracks. "That soon?"

She told herself she only imagined the note of distress in his voice. "I have to get back to work." That he could understand.

This time Daniel was the one to nod, but there didn't

seem to be any understanding in the gesture. "When I came into the ballroom a little while ago and looked up at the mezzanine and saw you standing there, it reminded me of when I walked into another party eight years ago. And suddenly, I felt…"

"What?" she asked breathlessly, feeling a little light-headed.

He hesitated, and when he spoke again, it wasn't to finish whatever he'd started to say. Instead, he said, "Marnie, the reason I left San Diego the way I did wasn't because I didn't care about you. It was because…" He took another step forward, something that brought his body within touching distance of her own. His eyes never leaving hers, he said, "It was because I cared about you too much."

Her mouth fell slightly open at that, but she said nothing, only returned his gaze without wavering, silently willing him to say more.

And, boy, did he say more. "That week was supposed to be the one I remembered all my life as the first great thing to happen to me as a horseman. Instead, I'll remember it as the first great thing to happen to me as a man. Because you were the first woman who ever made me think about something other than my work, Marnie. You're the *only* woman who ever made me think about something other than my work. And that was why I couldn't afford to see you again."

She swallowed against the sudden dryness in her

mouth. "Because your work was more important to you," she said shallowly.

He shook his head. "No. Because *you* were."

She closed her eyes at the admission, but had no idea what to say. When she opened them again, Daniel was still looking at her. Still standing within touching distance. Still not touching.

"I was so young, Marnie," he said. "We both were. And there was just so much between us. It scared the hell out of me. That was why I couldn't see you after the race, why I had to leave a letter in your mailbox. Because whenever I was with you, you made me forget things that I really needed to remember. I was afraid if I saw you again, physically *saw* you, and talked to you and touched you… I was afraid I'd never leave San Diego. And that would have meant I'd risk losing the one thing I knew was a sure thing—my work. With you…" Now he shook his head. "With you, I was never sure of anything."

He kept talking in the past tense, Marnie realized. As if what had happened between them was over completely. Was it because he felt that way? Or was it because he felt differently about his work now?

"That's funny," she said. But there wasn't an ounce of amusement in her voice. "Because with you, I was sure of everything. Who you were. Where we were headed. How I felt about you. How I thought you felt about me…"

"Marnie, the way I felt about you…"

He didn't—or perhaps couldn't—finish.

Not sure why she did it, Marnie lifted a hand to his face and cupped his jaw in her palm. "I felt that way, too." She started to tell him she still felt that way, but something stopped her. Maybe the realization that really, she wasn't sure how she felt about him now. There was still that rush of heat he'd always generated just by being close to her, and there was still that desire to share bits of herself with him. But there was something else now, too, something different, something uncertain, that hadn't been there before. Marnie didn't know yet if it was good or bad, so she didn't say anything more, only stroked the pad of her thumb over the ridge of his cheekbone and noted how the pulse at his throat jumped.

And the next thing she knew, she had pressed her mouth to his—or maybe he was the one who'd lowered his head to hers. No, she was up on tiptoe, so she must have been the one to start the kiss, and she had no desire to stop it. Evidently, neither did Daniel, because he caught her upper arms in his hands and pulled her higher still, turning his head to slant his mouth over hers, taking complete control. For a few moments, they vied for possession of the kiss. Then, as if of one mind, they surrendered to it. And let happen whatever was going to happen.

Marnie lifted her hands to Daniel's hair, threading her fingers through the silky tresses and grabbing great handfuls. Daniel dropped his arms around her waist, opening his hands at the small of her back, hooking his thumbs around her rib cage to delicately strum her torso.

She felt his hands at her waist, her hips, beneath the lower swells of her breasts. Then she felt them at her shoulders, pushing the straps of her dress down over her arms. He dipped his head to the delicate flesh he revealed, brushing his lips lightly across one shoulder, then along her collarbone, and into the hollow at the base of her throat. She tilted her head back to facilitate his explorations, one hand opening over his broad shoulder while the other tugged free the black tie at his collar. His top shirt buttons went next, until she could tuck her hand inside the crisp white fabric and spread her fingers over his heart, which was pounding as fiercely as her own.

His mouth returned to hers then, and he curved his hands over the swell of her fanny to push her pelvis against his. She felt him hard and heavy against her, ripening even more as their bodies connected. His hand was at the zipper of her gown, and hers was at the fastening of his trousers, when a bright light went on overhead.

"What in the bloody *hell* is going on in here?"

Marnie and Daniel sprang apart at the sound of the voice—Louisa Fairchild's. She stood in the doorway, a virago in red, hands on hips, feathers quivering angrily.

Chapter Nine

Marnie watched as Louisa took a few slow steps into the solarium, glancing from Marnie to Daniel and back again several times. She was doubtless taking in Daniel's loosened tie and unbuttoned shirt, and noticing how the straps of Marnie's dress had been pushed off her shoulders and down her arms, and the way the hair that had been swept up now tumbled free around her bare shoulders.

"Is this where all that money I'm sending to Division goes?" she demanded. "To bring you halfway around the world to visit your lover?"

Marnie did her best to look professional as she scooped her straps back up over her shoulders and began tucking her hair behind her ears. Oh, yeah. Easy to look professional doing that. Nevertheless, she tried to defend her behavior. "Louisa, that's not—"

"Don't you *Louisa* me, Miss Roberts." Louisa said. "Only my friends are allowed to call me by my given name. It's Miss Fairchild to you, you rotten Jezebel."

Marnie gaped at that. *Rotten Jezebel?* Where did Louisa Fairchild get off calling her that?

She did her best to remain calm. "Miss Fairchild. This isn't what you think it—"

"Is this why you were so het up to get me to drop the charges against Sam Whittleson?" she interrupted before Marnie could get the explanation out. "Because you've taken up with his son?"

"Of course not!" Marnie objected.

"Oh, right," Louisa said sarcastically. "I suppose you're going to tell me the two of you fell in love while you were plotting against an old woman."

Marnie colored at that. No, she wouldn't tell Louisa that, because it wasn't true. But she wasn't going to try to explain what she and Daniel were to each other, either. Her relationship—or whatever it was—with Daniel had nothing to do with her work for Louisa. "Miss Fairchild, Daniel and I knew each other a long time ago, and it was sheer coincidence that my client and his father were on the opposite side of this incident. When we saw each other again, we—"

But Louisa still wasn't listening. "I'm not your client anymore," she said. "You're fired, Miss Roberts."

"Miss Fairchild." This time it was Daniel who spoke.

He took a few steps forward and moved to stand in front of Marnie, as if he were shielding her.

"You're being unfair to Marnie," he said. "This wasn't her fault. It was mine."

"Oh, you were taking her against her will?" Louisa said sarcastically. "Then I should call the coppers. Like father like son. Criminals the both of you. Preying on innocent women."

"That's not true," Marnie said, stepping out from behind Daniel. She appreciated his chivalry, but she wasn't some quivering maiden, and this was as much her fault as it was his. "It's not true of Daniel or his father." More gently, she added, "And you know it."

Louisa pulled herself up at that. "What I know," she said, "is that I hired you to handle a dicey situation, and you ended up going over to the other side."

"No, you hired me to handle a difficult situation," Marnie said, "and I did it. I got the charges against you dropped and the gossip turned around. I've made sure you're well on your way to regaining your standing in the community. And most of all, I made sure this party tonight was a success so that you'd still be able to turn a hefty check over to your favorite charity."

"You didn't do any of that without me," Louisa said. "And not without whoring yourself to the other side, either."

Marnie felt Daniel stiffen beside her. Fearful that he might say something that would only make the situation worse, she curled her fingers around his forearm and said softly to Louisa, "That was unfair."

Louisa seemed surprised by the comment, having clearly expected a fight from Marnie or Daniel, or both. At Marnie's gentle admonishment, the fight seemed to go out of her. "You're fired," she said again, sounding tired now. "And you're not welcome in my house anymore. Pack your bags and get out. Now." Then she looked pointedly at Daniel and added, "You get out, too."

"But I'm a guest," he told her, his voice edged with not-so-subtle sarcasm. "You invited me into your home."

Worried his next comment was going to be something along the lines of *What are you going to do? Shoot me?*, Marnie squeezed his arm harder in warning.

Louisa narrowed her eyes at him, probably thinking the same thing Marnie was. All she said, however, was, "And I refuse to serve my guests when they're rotten scoundrels. And rotten Jezebels," she added, looking pointedly at Marnie again.

And then she was spinning around like an imperious top and heading out the door, her red dress flouncing and swishing behind her.

Still gripping Daniel's arm with one hand, Marnie dropped her head into the other. "Well, that went remarkably badly."

Daniel turned to pull her toward him and cupped his palm lightly over her nape. He didn't try to kiss her again, just studied her with those dark brown eyes she could lose herself in if she wasn't careful. "She's wrong about all of it, you know."

Marnie nodded. What she didn't tell him was that that was the main problem. Louisa hadn't been right about anything. Even the part about her and Daniel being in love. Especially that part.

But of all the myriad emotions tumbling through Marnie just then, the one she should have thought about most—concern over saving her job—was the one she cared about least. And the one she shouldn't be thinking about at all—her desire to be with Daniel—was the one she cared about most.

"This isn't good," she said aloud.

Daniel said nothing, only squeezed the back of her neck gently. "C'mon, I'll help you pack," he offered. "And you can stay at my dad's place tonight. We have plenty of room."

She started to decline, started to tell him she'd just go ahead and get a hotel in Sydney, since that was where she'd be catching her plane. Then she remembered it was going on midnight. "Thanks," she said. "I appreciate it. I'll get up early and drive into Sydney and find a hotel for tomorrow night."

"That won't be necessary."

"I have an early flight on Sunday," she lied. "It'll be more convenient."

"It's no problem if you want to stay at Dad's tomorrow, too."

"That's okay," she said wearily, exhaustion threatening to overcome her. "You've already done enough."

His eyes went flinty at her words and his mouth flattened into a tight line. The fingers on her neck fell away, and he took a step back. "I understand," he said tightly.

"Daniel, that's not what I meant," she quickly told him. "I was talking about giving me a place to stay for tonight."

He nodded, but she wasn't sure if he believed her or not. God, she wasn't sure of anything at the moment. Of Daniel's feelings or her own. All she knew was that, in forty-eight hours, she'd be back in her condo in San Diego. But where would Daniel be? Where did she want him to be? Where did she want to be herself?

She glanced at the door through which Louisa Fairchild had just huffed out. Then again, in forty-eight hours, Marnie might not have a job to go back to. She wouldn't be surprised if Louisa were in her office right now, phoning Division International, since the workday was still in full swing in California. She might be telling Hildy at this very moment what had happened.

Louisa's accusations might be a little over the top, but there was one thing Marnie wouldn't be able to deny. She had consorted with the opposition, and it would be difficult to prove there hadn't been a conflict of interest. It didn't matter that she had succeeded in doing what she'd come to Hunter Valley to do. In public relations, appearances were everything. And by all appearances, Marnie hadn't behaved professionally. Maybe not even ethically.

She wouldn't be surprised if she went into work next week only to have Hildy tell her to clean out her desk.

Great, she thought as she and Daniel made their way out of the solarium. This was just great. Not only was she losing Daniel for a second time, she was doubtless losing her job, too. She felt his hand at the small of her back as they passed through the solarium entrance, inhaled the spicy, intoxicating scent of him as he walked behind her.

And she knew without question which loss was going to stay with her the most.

Daniel stood in his father's kitchen Saturday morning, sipping his coffee and waiting for Marnie to come downstairs. He'd been up since six, and it was after nine now. She'd said she wanted to get an early start, but her definition of early must be different from his. Then again, the nine-to-five world she lived in operated by a different clock than the sunup-to-sundown one he inhabited, especially on the weekend. You could make people live by a specific workday. Horses? Not so easily.

He was swallowing the last of his third cup when his father came into the kitchen. Sam looked better today than he had yesterday. And yesterday he'd looked better than he had the day before that. Daniel was glad his father was in such good health. Most folks his age probably wouldn't have bounced back nearly as quickly from the kind of injury he'd sustained.

"Good morning," Daniel greeted his father.

Sam, still dressed in the striped pajama bottoms and white V-neck T-shirt he slept in, nodded at his son. "Mornin'," he drawled. Although he had lived all over the world, Sam's native Australian accent hadn't changed much. "You got Marnie off all right, I see. Crikey, I can't imagine why that girl got up so early. Even Sydney couldn't have been open by the time she got there. Especially on a Saturday."

Daniel threw his father a curious look. "What are you talking about? Marnie's still in bed." At his father's equally curious expression, he added, "Isn't she?"

"Well, if she is, then one of the horses must've taken some driving lessons while I was in hospital. I heard her car start up…oh, must've been five o'clock. It was after one when you two came in from Louisa's party last night. She couldn't have gotten more than a few hours' sleep."

If that much, Daniel thought. It was a two-hour drive to Sydney, much of it over dark country roads that she didn't know well. If she'd gotten up that early to drive to Sydney, it was because she hadn't wanted to risk running into him. Hadn't wanted to see him. Hadn't wanted to talk to him.

Not that he could really blame her. What had happened last night may very well have cost her her job at Division. Louisa would, without question, call Marnie's employer and complain about her behavior. Even after Marnie explained her side of things, Division would have to weigh the annual salary of one of its consultants with the annual retainer paid by one of their wealthiest clients—and the risk of that client bad-mouthing them to other clients. Marnie's spot at the end of the unemployment line was as good as reserved.

But even beyond that, he might very well have spooked her with all his talk about how important she'd been to him in San Diego. Marnie was focused on her career these days, just as Daniel had been eight years ago. Just as he was now, he hastily reminded himself. The last thing she probably wanted to hear was a hint he was carrying a torch for her.

Not that he was, he hastily amended. But what he'd said had probably made her uncomfortable. And then, for him to have kissed her the way he had... But she hadn't exactly put a stop to it the way she had that first night at her hotel. It was Louisa Fairchild who had done that. And who had fired Marnie and called her a Jezebel and...

Oh, jeez. He'd really done it this time. And trying to undo it might just make matters worse.

"Marnie said she wanted to get an early start," Daniel told his father lamely. "Guess she did that." And then, to change the subject, he quickly added, "You want coffee?"

"Too right I do," his father said. "And bacon and eggs and beans, thank you very much."

Daniel grinned halfheartedly. His father was doing better than he'd realized.

"I might try to check on the horses today," Sam added. "I miss those blokes."

"Just be careful, okay?"

"Aw, stop mollycoddling me, Danny. I feel fine. And

that nurse you hired to come in every day is like a drill sergeant. I'll be right as rain in no time."

Daniel reached behind himself for the coffeepot and poured his father a cup. As he handed it to him, though, he noted the circles under Sam's eyes, and how the creases in his forehead seemed deeper somehow. His body had taken a bullet, but he was recovering nicely from that. There just seemed to be more to his father's fatigue than the shooting. Sam didn't carry himself the way he used to, and his eyes were more often cast down to the floor than straight ahead. When he talked to Daniel, he never looked at him. His spirit just didn't seem to be as bright, as alive, as it used to be.

He remembered again the bank balances that had seemed too low, and he wondered if his father had hit a rough patch without telling Daniel about it. The Thoroughbred business was generally a strong one, and his father was a trainer who'd built his career—and Whittleson Stud—by being in high demand. But any business could reach a point where things slowed down, even temporarily.

"Dad?" he said as his father took the cup from him. "Is everything okay on the station? I mean, financially, are you all right?"

The cup slipped right out of his father's hand, thumping onto the linoleum without breaking, but spewing coffee everywhere. Immediately, Daniel grabbed a dish towel from the counter and bent to mop up the mess, catching most of it before it got too far.

"What are you talking about?" his father asked. "Of course everything's all right on the station. Why would you think I'm having money trouble?"

There was an edge of desperation in his voice that Daniel had never heard before, and that, more than anything else, told him something was wrong. But before he could probe further, his cell phone rang. He rose and snatched it up from the counter, thinking he'd call back whoever it was. But when he saw that it was Thomas Preston—and that Thomas was supposed to be flying over the continental United States at the moment—Daniel flipped open the phone to answer.

Before he could get out a greeting, Thomas barked, "Daniel? It's Thomas. We need you in Sydney right now."

"Sydney?" Daniel echoed. "But you're supposed to be on a charter headed to New York."

"Yeah, well, there's a problem with that."

"I'll say. You're still in Sydney."

"Brent called just as we were leaving Louisa's last night with some *very* troubling news."

"Troubling enough to make you miss the Belmont Stakes?" Daniel asked. "'Cause there's no way you're going to see Melanie take the Triple Crown now."

"Melanie won't be taking the Triple Crown," Thomas said flatly. "Not this year, anyway."

Something in Daniel's belly knotted tight at the statement. "What are you talking about? What's happened to Melanie?"

"Melanie's fine," Thomas told him.

Then something must have happened to Leopold's Legacy. "Legacy?" he asked.

"Legacy is fine, too," Thomas told him. "At least where his health is concerned."

"Then why aren't they going to be winning the Belmont Stakes?"

"That's why we need you here in Sydney," Thomas said cryptically. "Jenna and I rescheduled the charter from last night and are headed back to Kentucky this afternoon instead. Is your dad doing well enough that you can come back with us?"

"Whoa, whoa, whoa," Daniel protested. "What the hell is going on?"

"Look, just come to Sydney as soon as you can. And if you can be away from your dad, come ready to travel. I'll tell you what's going on when you get here."

Marnie was sitting in a Sydney coffee shop, trying not to think about how, this time yesterday, she was gainfully employed by one of the largest public relations firms in the United States, and that now, thanks to the phone call she'd just had with Hildy, she was little more than an unemployment statistic, when her cell phone rang again.

Although the number showing wasn't one she recognized, she opened her phone. Before she could get out a greeting, Daniel's voice on the other end, terse and demanding, said, "Where are you?"

She'd known he wasn't going to be thrilled about the

way she'd ducked him by leaving so early, but this was a little uncalled-for. Not quite able to hide her annoyance at his tone, she snapped, "Standing in the unemployment line."

That seemed to do the trick, because he said nothing for a moment. Then, "I'm sorry for bellowing," he apologized in a much gentler voice. "I'm not having a good morning."

That made two of them.

"Are you really unemployed?" he asked.

"I am," she told him. "I just had a long talk with my boss…excuse me, *ex*-boss…who'd had a long talk with Louisa. Long story short, I'm supposed to clean out my desk as soon as I get back to San Diego."

"I'm sorry," he said again. And somehow, she got the feeling he was talking about a lot more than her job.

"Yeah, me, too," she replied, hoping he got the feeling she was talking about a lot more than her job.

"So where are you really?" he asked.

"In a coffee shop across the street from the Four Seasons Hotel in Sydney," she told him. She'd figured she might as well go out with a bang, staying at the luxury hotel her last night in Australia, but she wouldn't be able to check in for hours. Fortunately, she'd brought a book and had decided to camp out here at the coffee shop until she could go up to her room.

"Is it the coffee shop called Antoinette's?" Daniel asked.

"How did you know that?" she said.

"I'm looking at it from Thomas and Jenna's window."

His answer explained nothing, only opened up a host of questions. "I thought they were leaving last night."

"So did they. Change of plans."

"Why? And what does any of this have to do with me? Daniel, what's going on?"

There was a moment of silence, then he said, "I need you." Just as her heart was beginning to flutter hopefully, he amended, "I mean, *we* need you. The Prestons and I. Tom and Jenna want to hire you. For PR."

"Why would the Kentuckian Prestons want to hire an unemployed San Diego PR person?" Marnie asked. "Especially when they can find a perfectly good one in Lexington or Louisville who didn't just nearly cost her firm one of their wealthiest clients while she was supposed to be making inroads into an entirely new market?"

There was another moment's pause, then he said, "Because the unemployed San Diego PR person came highly recommended, that's why."

"By who?"

"By me."

Before Marnie had time to think about the implications of that, he hurried on. "There's a huge problem with one of their horses, and the media are going to get hold of the story any minute, and it's going to be a PR nightmare. They need someone they can trust *now.* I told them that not only could they could trust you, but that you convinced both Louisa Fairchild and my father— the two most stubborn people in Hunter Valley—to drop the charges against each other. They agree with me that anyone who can do that can do just about anything. So what do you say, Marnie? You need a job?"

More than just about anything, she thought. "What's the PR nightmare?"

"I can tell you about it in ten minutes. Maybe five, if you're finished with your coffee. Do you want the job or not?"

"I want the job," she said. "I'll be right there."

No matter how big a PR nightmare it was, it couldn't be any worse than the nightmare of going back to San Diego. Especially without Daniel.

Chapter Ten

A few hours later, Marnie was sitting in the back of a chartered jet with Daniel and Thomas and Jenna, rubbing her temples and munching an antacid, trying to make sense of what they were telling her. The minute she'd entered their hotel room, they were upon her like a pack of wolves, all of them talking at once, and none of them making any sense. Most of that early conversation had been about how grateful they were to her for taking on the job, and how lucky they were that she was here, and that they had to hurry to catch the jet they'd chartered because they hadn't wanted to wait for a commercial flight—or risk running into a member of the media upon landing in Lexington. They'd assured her they would get her caught up to speed once they were aboard the jet, where they could speak at length.

Now that they were all settled on board, however, the three of them were making even less sense than they had at the hotel. Something about their horse Leopold's Legacy and DNA testing and the Jockey Association. That was about all that Marnie had been able to pick out of the jumble of conversation, since much of it was ricocheting between the three of them.

"Stop!" she finally shouted into the cacophony.

Immediately, they did, turning to stare at her curiously, almost as if they'd forgotten she was there.

"Start at the beginning," she said.

All three began talking at once.

"One of you," she corrected, raising her voice to be heard. And because she was playing favorites, she pointed at Daniel. "You," she said. "Tell me what's going on. Speak slowly and as if I know nothing about Thoroughbred racing. I may have grown up around horses, but my family raised hunter-jumpers. And that's a whole 'nother ball game."

Daniel nodded. "Then you don't know about the DNA registry kept by the Jockey Association."

She shook her head. "Not really, no. I know all Thoroughbreds have to be registered with the Association, but that's about it."

He blew out a long breath. "By the time we get to Kentucky, Marnie, you're going to be an expert on everything that has anything to do with the Jockey Association and the ITRF."

It took her only a second to figure out the acronym: International Thoroughbred Racing Federation.

"Brent Preston got word yesterday in Kentucky that Leopold's Legacy, winner of both the Kentucky Derby and the Preakness," he elaborated unnecessarily, "the Preston family's pride and joy, the veritable jewel in the Quest Stables crown, isn't the horse we've all thought he was. He may not even be a true Thoroughbred. And if that's the case—and we still aren't accepting that it is—then Quest Stables is in a whole heap of trouble."

"I don't understand," Marnie said. "Isn't the breeding of Thoroughbreds closely monitored?"

"When Legacy was bred," Daniel explained, "his dam—that would be his mama…"

"I know what dams and sires are," Marnie told him. "You don't have to lower the bar that much."

He dipped his head in acknowledgment. "His dam, whose name was Courtin' Cristy, was covered by Apollo's Ice."

Before he could ask, she said, "And yes, I know that *covered* means they had sex."

He grinned at that, but sobered quickly. "Brent Preston and Carter Phillips, the Prestons' veterinarian, watched the covering at Angelina Stud Farm. The Jockey Association doesn't recognize any artificially inseminated Thoroughbreds, only those conceived through live cover. And Apollo's Ice was the *only* horse to cover her. When Legacy's birth was registered with the Jockey Association, Courtin' Cristy and Apollo's Ice were listed as his dam and sire in accordance with all the rules and regulations. There's no question Cristy is the dam—Legacy's birth was witnessed by a half-dozen people. But his daddy, now, that's where the problem comes in."

"How so?" Marnie asked.

"This is where it gets complicated," Daniel told her. "It's always been a rule with the Jockey Association that within thirty days after Thoroughbreds are born, they're required to have blood drawn to check for disease. Nowadays, with DNA testing available, it's also routine to have their parentage checked, as well, to ensure potential buyers that they're getting what they paid for. When that test was done for Legacy, everything checked out. But a while back, the Jockey Association underwent a massive computer system replacement, and all the data had to be reentered. When Legacy's information was reentered and compared with the backup data, they discovered there was a discrepancy."

That didn't sound good. "What kind of discrepancy?"

"In the live data—that would be the original information recorded about Legacy's birth—the sire was listed as Apollo's Ice, just as it was supposed to be. But in the backup data, his sire was listed as Unknown."

"How could that be?"

"We don't know. We're convinced there's no way another horse could have covered Courtin' Cristy and sired a foal prior to Apollo's Ice, but the DNA proves that another, mystery horse sired Legacy. The Association is investigating, trying to figure out how there could be such a discrepancy, but so far, they're coming up empty."

As Marnie had just told them, she knew little about Thoroughbred racing. However, she was familiar enough with the equestrian world to know it placed a lot of stock in lineage. A horse's bloodline was everything. If that bloodline couldn't be established, then...

Well, she wouldn't go so far as to say the horse was nothing. But in the world of Thoroughbreds, where horses were sometimes bought and sold for millions of dollars, bloodlines were worth a fortune.

"So what does that mean for Quest Stables, if Legacy's paternity is unknown?" she asked.

"The fallout could be catastrophic," Jenna said. "If we can't prove that Leopold's Legacy is a Thoroughbred—if we never identify the sire, or if we do and the sire turns out not to be a registered Thoroughbred—then Legacy will be stripped of all his winnings, including the Derby and the Preakness. Meaning all that money— millions of dollars, Marnie—will have to be returned."

"But as bad as that is," Thomas added, "believe it or not, it's not the worst of it. With Legacy's bloodline in question, the stable's reputation and livelihood are at stake. The vast majority of the horses at Quest are boarded there for training. People pay a premium for those services, because Quest's reputation—until now—has been one of the best in the business. If

Quest's integrity is in question, those owners will almost certainly pull their animals from our farm and put them somewhere else, and that's going to amount to a lot of the money we depend on to operate."

"And it gets worse still," Daniel said. "The Jockey Association may insist all other horses at Quest be tested, to make sure this is an isolated incident. And if it isn't, that'll be the end of Quest. No one will want to come near us." His expression was grim as he added, "Even if it *is* an isolated incident, the Jockey Association will recall Leopold's Legacy's status, and all of the local and regional racing commissions would most likely ban all horses that are majority owned by Quest from racing in North America as well, until the test results are in. And the testing could take months. If that happened, it would be yet another huge financial hit for the stable."

Thomas rubbed his forehead. "This is going to kill my father. He built Quest from the ground up, dedicated his whole life to it. If we lose it…" He dropped his hand to his side. "I don't want to think about the effect it will have on him."

"It's bad enough we had to pull Legacy from the Belmont Stakes," Jenna said. "Poor Hugh was so excited about the prospect of having a Triple Crown winner. And Melanie's heartbroken she got as close as she did and won't be able to go all the way."

"Has Leopold's Legacy been disqualified from the Belmont Stakes?" Marnie asked, alarmed. "Has it already gone that far?"

Jenna shook her head. "No, but I think it would be very bad form for us to run him, knowing what we do about the DNA test. Not to mention the fact that, depending on how this plays out, if Legacy won, and we never discover his true sire, that would be another win he'd be stripped of, and it would just make things more difficult."

"Don't even talk like that, Jenna," Thomas said. "We *will* find out who his sire is, and it *will* be a Thoroughbred, and we *will* bounce back from this."

Jenna smiled weakly at her husband. "You're right, of course."

Funny, though, Marnie thought, she didn't sound anywhere near as confident as her words.

"We didn't give a very good explanation to the track for our decision," Jenna said, turning back to Marnie, "and that's sure to spread gossip and speculation. But what else could we do? The newspapers are bound to get wind of this, and if we let Legacy run in the race after knowing the results of the DNA test, it would just feed the image that we can't be trusted and are running a shady operation."

"Good call," Marnie said. "It would have been my first recommendation to you from a PR standpoint. I'm glad we're already on the same page."

"Melanie and Robbie are on their way home with Legacy as we speak," Jenna told her. "They should be arriving at Quest about the same time we are."

Marnie nodded, but her thoughts had already moved on. "There's got to be an explanation for all of this."

"Well, we better find it quick," Daniel said, "because the clock is ticking. For every minute that this goes on, the stable's credibility is on the line."

Marnie's mind was already teeming with ideas, but she was sure there was going to be lots more she needed to learn and consider before she could outline a good PR plan.

And as Marnie looked at Daniel and listened to him talking with Jenna and Thomas, she realized it wasn't just the PR plan she was thinking about. Because without even meaning to, she'd saved room in her brain— and her heart—for Daniel, too.

They had another chance, after all, she thought. The question was, would either of them take it?

Marnie had visited Kentucky once before, years ago, when she was still in high school, for a horse show in which she'd been competing. But she hadn't spent much time outside Louisville. As Brent Preston drove them toward Quest in one of the stable's big SUVs, Marnie watched the swiftly passing landscape and felt herself relax a little.

It was gorgeous countryside, hills rolling like green velvet beneath a sky the color of a robin's egg that was streaked with gauzy white clouds. The midmorning sun was still low in the sky, but its warmth streamed happily through the vehicle's windows. Coming on the heels of Australia's winter, the surroundings looked exuberantly lush and vivid. The temperature, too, was more agreeable to her Southern California sensibilities, and in spite of the work she knew lay ahead, she was glad to be here.

She closed her eyes as the SUV rolled down the two-lane blacktop, exhaustion overcoming her. She'd been surprised, on the flight, to discover she really wasn't as unhappy about losing her position at Division International as she would have thought. Now she wouldn't have to babysit the rich, pampered clients on her list who should have grown up a long time ago.

Maybe when she got back to San Diego, she'd think about starting her own firm. She could probably woo away the accounts she liked from her Division list—in fact, Division would probably cut them all loose without Marnie there, anyway, since those clients weren't huge moneymakers for the company. And she could actively seek new accounts from groups and individuals who did good work and made the world better in some small— or even large—way.

People like the Prestons, for example. They were good, hardworking people who were trying to preserve both a family business and a family tradition. She intended to work just as hard as they did to make sure everything worked out for them. And if she did her job well enough, perhaps they would even keep her on. They could be the first of her new clients. That would be like a dream come true….

"Home sweet home," she heard Brent say.

Opening her eyes, Marnie realized they had arrived at Quest Stables. She must have dozed off for the last part of the drive. She inhaled a deep breath and started to stretch her arms out wide, but instead gently bumped Daniel, who was seated in the very back seat with her. When she looked over, she saw that he, too, had nodded off, but he was still sleeping. His head was tilted against the window, and his arms were crossed over his chest. He'd shed his sweater at the Lexington airport, and his broad shoulders and bunched biceps strained against the burgundy fabric of his T-shirt. Dark hair sprang from beneath the collar; his throat and the lower half of his face were shadowed by a day's growth of dark beard, and his even-darker lashes—unbelievably long for a man—fluttered over his rugged cheekbones.

He was dreaming, she realized with a smile. She wondered what about.

Leaning across the seat, she curved her hand over his arm, trying not to notice how warm and strong it felt beneath her fingertips. "Hey, Sleeping Beauty," she whispered. "Time to turn back into a pumpkin."

Okay, so she was mixing up her fairy tales. The way he looked at the moment, she was lucky she could remember anything at all.

He didn't respond at first, just continued to breathe deeply, his chest rising and falling with each slow exhalation. So she unbuckled her seat belt and scooted across the long bench seat until she was sitting right beside him.

"Hey," she said a little louder. "We're home, Daniel. Rise and shine."

He inhaled deeply and turned to face her, but his eyes remained closed. After a small hesitation, she lifted her hand to his shoulder—it was even warmer and stronger than his arm had been, but she tried not to notice that, either—and gave him a soft shake. Finally, his eyes fluttered open, and his gaze immediately fell on hers. He smiled—the exact same smile she'd seen from him so often in Del Mar, the one she'd missed so much for eight unbearably long years—and murmured, "Marnie." He spoke her name the way he had before, his voice full of warmth and serenity and affection. And for one second—one tiny, delirious, wonderful second—she was overcome with the same love she had felt for him back then. The giddy, glowing, tumble-in-the-stomach kind of love, full of wonder and hope and possibility and the marvel of realizing how incredibly lucky she had been to meet him when she did.

Then his eyes focused, and he realized where he was. And then his smile, though it didn't go away, changed, and was suddenly tempered by what must have been his memory of the circumstances of their return. He sat up straighter, unbuckled his seat belt, scrubbed a hand through his hair and turned his wrist to check his watch.

"Man, I was out," he said. "I can never sleep in cars."

She turned to look out the window on her side of the car, pretending to take in her surroundings, hoping her face hadn't revealed anything of what she'd been feeling in the wake of that momentary smile. Her eyes watered against the sunlight—surely that was the reason—so she said something about having slept herself and swiped her fingers over her eyes to clear them.

"C'mon, you two," Brent called from outside. "Time to be out and about. It's going on noon. Jeez, you'd think you people just flew halfway around the world or something."

He was grinning at them, and Marnie couldn't help but grin back. Like the rest of the Prestons, Brent was impossibly handsome, with his father's dark hair and his mother's blue eyes. He looked to be in his mid-thirties, was tall like his father, wore his hair a little on the long side, and was dressed in well-worn blue jeans and a short-sleeved denim work shirt. Marnie had learned on the flight from Australia that he was the Preston's head breeder and had appointed himself to head up the farm's task force tackling the DNA mystery. She made a mental note to meet with him as soon as possible.

As Marnie climbed out of the SUV behind Daniel, two little girls came running up from nowhere—identical twins, Marnie saw as they drew closer—chorusing, "Daddy! Daddy! Daddy!" They both grabbed Brent around the waist—though they were barely tall enough—and began to hug him hard, giggling gleefully at their father's return. He laughed, too, and dropped a hand to ruffle their hair, then bent and kissed the crowns of their heads, first one, then the other.

"Honestly," Jenna said beside her, smiling gently. "You'd think Katie and Rhea hadn't seen their father for a month instead of a morning. Since their mother passed away, they don't want him out of their sight."

Before Marnie could respond, Jenna turned to her and smiled a sad, tired smile. "You look beat. Didn't you get any sleep on the jet?"

Marnie shook her head. "I can never sleep on planes, trains or automobiles."

She could only sleep in SUVs when Daniel was sleeping beside her, she thought. But there was no reason Jenna had to know that. Still, it was going to take a while to readjust her inner clock to the Eastern time zone. She'd just been getting acclimated to Hunter Valley time when she'd left. Now she'd have to overcompensate for the three-hour difference between here and San Diego.

Jenna patted her on the shoulder comfortingly. "I called ahead and had one of the empty cabins made up for you. It's near Daniel's. He can show you the way."

"Thanks," Marnie told her. "I appreciate it."

"Both of you should try to take a nap. We can all get together this afternoon with Brent to talk some more about Leopold's Legacy."

"Me, too," said a young woman who'd come to greet them. She was a few inches taller than Marnie, very pretty, with huge brown eyes and rich auburn hair pulled back in a ponytail. She wore blue jeans that had definitely seen better days, and an oversize T-shirt, emblazoned with the logo of a tractor company, that wasn't in much better shape. "I'm helping Brent out with the investigation. Doing the gopher work for him."

She took a few long strides toward Jenna and gave her a quick hug in greeting. But it was the kind of hug men usually practiced, a little awkward, with a swift pat on the back, then an immediate step backward, as if she was fearful someone might read something into the gesture that wasn't there. Jenna, Marnie saw, had tried to hold on a little longer, but when the young woman sprang backward, Jenna contented herself instead with tucking an errant strand of the woman's hair behind her ear.

At first Marnie thought this must be Melanie Preston, but Jenna greeted her as Audrey. Then she turned to Marnie and said, "Marnie Roberts, this is Audrey Griffin. She's one of our grooms and our expert horseshoer."

"Really?" Marnie asked. "That's kind of unusual work for a woman, isn't it?"

She hadn't meant anything by the remark—in her experience, horseshoers were generally men. But Audrey's chin went up defensively at the question. "Not anymore," she said.

Jenna turned to Marnie. "Don't even go there," she said softly with a smile, but still loud enough that she clearly meant for Audrey to hear. "I've tried to get her to leave the horseshoes behind for office work instead, but she'll have no part of it." Jenna looked at Audrey again and raised a comically critical brow. "I've tried to get her to put a dress on from time to time, too, but she won't have any part of that, either."

Audrey wrinkled her nose in disgust. "Why would I

need to wear a dress around horses? They don't care what I look like."

Jenna gave a much put-upon sigh. "I know, dear," she said. "That's the problem."

Audrey looked confused at that, but Jenna quickly turned back to Marnie and Daniel. "Why don't we meet around three at the big house?" she said. "That'll give all of us a chance to get a few hours' sleep before we put our heads together."

"Sounds good," Daniel told her. "Which cabin is Marnie in?"

"Number five," Jenna told him. "The key should be in the mailbox."

"That's right next door to me," he said. And Marnie told herself she was just imagining his slightly troubled tone.

Jenna nodded. "Is that a problem?" Evidently, she'd detected the note of concern in his voice, too.

"No, of course not," he replied. "I just thought…"

"What?" But it wasn't Jenna who spoke this time. It was Marnie.

Daniel turned to look at her, his eyes shadowed by lack of sleep. "Nothing," he said. "C'mon. I'll show you the way."

Chapter Eleven

Daniel felt better after getting a few hours of sleep, but he was still a little muddleheaded as he went to get Marnie for their three o'clock meeting at the big house. Then again, he suspected the muddle wasn't due simply to a lack of sleep. A lot of it had to do with Marnie's presence in the cabin next to his.

He still wasn't sure what had made him recommend her to the Prestons when it became clear they needed a professional to help them preserve Quest's image in light of what was sure to become a scandal of international proportions. Marnie had been right when she said they could have hired someone closer to home. Hell, they could have hired someone who specialized in PR for the Thoroughbred industry, for that matter.

Then again, having met the Prestons—and knowing Daniel—she might feel as if she had a bit of a personal stake in this, and personal commitment was worth just as much as professional connections. Maybe even more. He'd wanted to be sure whoever Jenna and Thomas hired could be trusted implicitly. Someone who was inherently decent. And Marnie Roberts was that. She'd been decent to him, even after the way he'd abandoned her in San Diego, and she'd been decent to his father, never capitalizing on his actions in the shooting incident the way she could have. She may have threatened to vilify his father, but she'd never carried through, even though that would have furthered her efforts in exonerating her client.

He hadn't suggested Marnie to the Prestons because he still felt guilty over what had happened in San Diego. And it wasn't because he hadn't been ready to part ways with Marnie. It was because he knew she could get the job done. Because her work was important to her. As important as his was to him.

And why did that realization bother him so much? he wondered. Why shouldn't Marnie's work be as important to her as his was to him? Why shouldn't she crave success the same way that he did?

Jet lag, he told himself. Jet lag had scrambled his brains. That was the only reason he felt as befuddled as he did where Marnie was concerned. A midafternoon nap wasn't nearly enough to get him caught up.

The five cabins on the Quest Stables property were

virtually identical on the outside, one-bedroom, barn-red frame structures with small front porches and tiny, but tidy, yards. Most were used as guesthouses or for senior employees, and Daniel had opted to live in one full-time when he came to work at Quest. He'd liked the idea of not having to get up and drive to work every morning, but, even more, he'd liked the feeling of being a part of the family that was Quest Stables. Jenna mothered him the same way she did everyone else on the farm, and the Prestons' sons felt almost like the brothers Daniel had often wished for as a boy.

Still, he'd be lying if he didn't confess that there had been times lately—even before going to Australia—when he had found himself wanting something more than his life at Quest. His goal had always been to have his own farm one day, and he still had his eye on that. But even thinking about that now didn't fill him with the sense of purpose it once had. Since going to Australia, he'd felt restless and edgy and unsettled. Part of that, he was sure, was due to his father's injury and the more recent problem with Leopold's Legacy, but most of it, he had to admit, was because of Marnie's reentry into his life.

Just what was he expecting? he asked himself as he approached her cabin. Unfortunately, he could no more answer that question than he could any of the others he'd asked himself since his return. So, like the others, he pushed it to the back of his brain and did his best not to think about it.

The small front porch of Marnie's cabin had been

made cozy with potted plants and two Adirondack chairs. And although the inside would be laid out the same as his—a small living room immediately inside, a single bedroom beyond, a galley kitchen to the right and a bathroom to the left—the decor would be different. Jenna wanted all of her guests to feel special and had furnished each of the cabins in a different style.

Marnie's cabin was the French Provincial one, Daniel recalled with a smile as he rapped on the front door. Full of girlie white furniture and flower prints and Paris bistro accouterments. Fortunately, when Jenna had assigned a cabin to Daniel, she'd given him the one furnished in Montana Manly. It was full of rough-hewn pine furniture and plaid.

When Marnie answered his knock, she looked a little fresher than she had earlier. The purple smudges under her eyes were fainter, and the hair that had been tousled from sleep last time he'd seen her was tamed—though, now that he thought about it, he actually kind of preferred the sleep-rumpled look. She'd changed her clothes, too, and wore blue jeans and a white, sleeveless, button-up shirt. But the wholesome, down-on-the-farm image was dispelled when he noted the expensive-looking leather portfolio she clutched in one hand, because it reminded him of her real reason for being here. Until he saw that, he'd kind of felt as though he was coming to pay a social call on her—though why he would feel that way, he couldn't say. Another one of those questions without an answer.

"Feeling better?" he asked by way of a greeting.

She nodded. "It's amazing what a few hours of sleep can do."

"Yeah, but it'll only last a few hours," he said. "By bedtime, you'll be exhausted again."

"Goes with the job," she told him as she stepped out and closed the door behind her. "I don't travel a lot, but it's not unusual for me to have to make cross-country trips at a moment's notice. You'd think my body would be acclimated to sudden changes in time, but noooo." She smiled. "One reason I prefer to stay rooted in one place."

Daniel nodded. He preferred that, too. He just wished he could find the one place he wanted to stay rooted in forever. Quest was great, and he loved his work here, but when he looked down the road ten years—hell, even five years—he couldn't see himself still training horses for the Prestons.

"Will you stay in San Diego now, with the job at Division gone?" he asked her as they began the walk to the big house.

"I honestly don't know," she said. "I really haven't thought about it. Now that my folks are living up in Sonoma, I could move north. I do still have a lot of clients in Southern California, but I could easily handle those from elsewhere. It might be kind of fun to have my own firm. But that's a lot of work." She glanced over at Daniel with an obviously halfhearted smile. "Then again, what else do I have, right?" Before he could reply, she hurried on, "Right now, all I can focus on is doing what I can for the Prestons. I'll think about the rest of it later."

The Prestons were all present when Daniel and Marnie entered the kitchen, including Hugh, who sat at the kitchen table with his Irish wolfhound, Seamus, at his feet. The room was cavernous and would have been overwhelming were it not for the cozy touches Jenna had added, giving it the feel of a Tuscany *cucina*. The walls were painted terra-cotta, the cabinets were sage and the floors were creamy, weathered tile. Colorful bits of pottery brightened every available space, and the appliances—all state-of-the-art—were unobtrusively tucked into nooks and crannies, maintaining the Old World feel.

Fortunately, one of those appliances was a coffeemaker that had been freed from its hiding place. Making himself at home as he always did in the Prestons' house, Daniel poured two cups—one for himself and one for Marnie. She accepted it from him gratefully, closing her eyes to inhale the rich aroma before lifting the cup to her mouth for a long, leisurely sip.

She had been like that in San Diego, he remembered. A sensualist in every respect. She'd loved bright colors and textured fabrics, had filled her apartment with scented candles and lively music and gourmet foods. Whenever they'd entered a room, she'd had to stop for a few seconds to look around, to absorb and appreciate her surroundings. That week Daniel had spent with her, he'd seen the world in a way he'd never seen it before. Through the eyes of someone who loved living in it, someone for whom the simple act of being alive brought great joy. He wondered what had happened to that person, why she had replaced that zest for life with a compulsion to work. Sure, her parents' loss of income had put her in a tight spot, but there had to be more to it than that.

Then Marnie opened her eyes again, connecting with his, and the smile she'd had on her face while enjoying the smell of the coffee fell a little bit. And that was when Daniel knew. That was when he realized what had happened to her. He understood why she no longer wore the bright clothes and why she wasn't as quick to smile as she used to be. He knew why she was different.

It wasn't because of the financial loss her family had endured. She had said her parents seemed happier now than they'd ever been. It was because of him. Because of what he'd done eight years ago. When he'd walked out of Marnie's life the way he had, he'd taken Marnie with him. Or at least that vibrant, laughing, loving part of her. The soul of her. The spirit.

No wonder he'd never been able to forget her, he thought. She'd been with him all the time.

Oh, man. He was an even bigger jerk than he'd realized.

Before he had a chance to ponder that further, Brent called the meeting to order. Everyone joined Hugh at the big kitchen table that was so seldom used for eating meals. Thomas went to the head, with Jenna on one side and Andrew on the other, and everyone else grabbed the closest chair.

At thirty-six, Andrew was the oldest Preston offspring, the business manager of Quest Stables. Like his brothers, he topped six feet and had the signature dark hair and blue eyes. Melanie, the only Preston daughter, sat beside Andrew. She was the solitary blonde in the family and had inherited her mother's petite frame. Except that, at barely five feet, she was even shorter than her mother. Robbie, the youngest, sat beside his sister and across from his parents.

After introducing Marnie to everyone and explaining her role in the situation, Brent got right to the point.

"So far, there's been nothing said in the press about Legacy's questionable paternity," he began. "Which means, if we hurry, we can create the initial spin and set the mood for the way it's reported. Not that there's going to be any *good* way to say that our most famous horse, the one everybody's talking about, has recently been discovered to have what might very well be a corrupted bloodline."

"There's no way Legacy's bloodline is corrupted," Melanie stated adamantly. "Maybe his sire isn't Apollo's Ice, but it *is* a Thoroughbred. A damned good one, too. No animal could perform the way Legacy does without premium lines."

A general murmur of agreement went around the table.

"The first thing we need to do," Brent continued, "is put together a press release. It would probably even be good to have a press conference. Marnie—" he looked at her "—will be in charge of that," he told the group.

"Let's start locally, with the sportscasters and sports-writers on a list I prepared earlier." He passed it across the table to Marnie, who picked it up and scanned the names. "These are men and women who have always been good to Quest," he told her, "and they're fair-minded people, so I think they'll be the right ones to break the news. Then we can alert the ITRF cable channel, ESPN, all of those guys. Broadcast networks last, I think, since they'll have the least interest."

"Before we do any of that," Marnie said, looking up, "you might want to consider telling anyone affiliated with Quest who's going to be affected by this. The people who board their animals here, the ones who've hired the services of your trainers, the ones who've paid stud fees for Leopold's Legacy. Especially the last."

Brent's features went a little slack. "You're talking about hundreds of people, Marnie. And it's Sunday. A lot of people will be out visiting neighbors and won't be home. There's no way we can notify everyone before tomorrow morning. As it is, I'm holding my breath that no one gets wind of this before then. There's been a massive amount of speculation already about why we pulled Legacy from the Belmont Stakes. We said he suffered a superficial injury that would prevent him from running yesterday, but there's still been plenty of gossip."

"I understand," Marnie said. "But if your clients hear about this on the news instead of from you, they're *not* going to be happy. You want me to spin this, I'm telling you those people need to be notified before you go public."

He leaned back in his chair. "You're right. I'll get Audrey on that."

Thomas said, "If she can organize the names and phone numbers, then you and I and Jenna, Andrew, Robbie and Melanie can make the actual phone calls." He looked at the other family members. "I think our clients should hear it from us."

The other Prestons nodded their agreement.

"Even if we can't get in touch with people right away," Thomas said, "we can leave messages to return our call, and that will let them know we tried to reach them before we went to the press."

Brent nodded. "Audrey offered to help out on this thing. She can pull the information from our database. It won't take any time at all. Tonight and tomorrow morning, we'll make the calls. Tomorrow afternoon, just after lunch, we go public with this—hopefully before anyone else."

"So just how bad is this going to get?" Daniel asked.

"It could get very bad," Brent said. "And we should think about all worst-case scenarios when we strategize."

They did that and more, with Marnie interjecting pertinent observations where necessary, and asking questions whenever she needed clarification on something. Daniel watched and listened to her as she took notes and brainstormed ideas and promised to have a press release available by the end of the evening. She also coached everyone involved on the best ways to approach both the media and the Quest clientele, and told the Prestons what to tell their other employees—right down to the stall muckers—about how to respond to the questions they were bound to be asked by everyone from members of the media to their Great-Aunt Viola about what was happening at Quest.

She was cool, professional, and to the point, Daniel noted as he watched her. And damn, she was good. By the time the meeting drew to a close, it was almost as if she, even more than Brent and Thomas, had taken control of the situation.

Clearly, she took her job very seriously. Clearly, her job was extremely important to her. Clearly, she felt as strongly about her work as Daniel did.

Or as Daniel had. Because he was beginning to understand now why he'd felt so restless since Marnie reentered his life. The problem now was that Daniel didn't fear her presence there. He didn't worry that she might overshadow his career. Didn't worry that she might become more important to him. He was beginning to think she'd never stopped being more important. Only now, he thought he could handle it. Now, he was confident enough in his work to know he could allow distractions. Distractions like a relationship. Distractions like Marnie.

But it was Marnie who now put her work first. She was the one who had no room for him. And it was Daniel who had paved the way for that eight years ago in San Diego.

* * *

Over the next few days, everyone worked hard trying to solve the mystery of how a stallion other than Apollo's Ice could have bred with Courtin' Cristy during the time frame when Leopold's Legacy was conceived. Brent and Thomas and Daniel began to draw blood for DNA testing from all the Quest horses that could be potential candidates, in the hope that one of those Thoroughbreds was the real sire. If so, there was a chance—they hoped—that the Jockey Association would give them permission to amend Legacy's registration in the stud book. As long as his sire was a registered Thoroughbred, he would still be considered a Thoroughbred himself, and couldn't be stripped of his winnings or status. He would also still have champion bloodlines that would make the stud fees paid for his services to date legitimate.

But it was rough going, and everyone's nerves were stretched thin. It was hard to stay upbeat when every time they turned on the TV or opened the newspaper or an industry journal, they read something about Legacy, or Quest, or the Preston family itself, often unfavorable. Every employee suffered, because, as Marnie had cautioned them, anyone affiliated with Quest seemed to be under indictment.

Finally, in an attempt to alleviate the quickly declining morale at the stable, Thomas decreed that Quest Stables would host a barbecue to end all barbecues, the mother of all cookouts. It was the remedy he always fell back on in times of turmoil. Cooking and eating brought people together, so a big barbecue, he reasoned, couldn't help but lift everyone's spirits.

Three days after they'd held the PR powwow in the Preston kitchen, the same group gathered there again. Only this time it was to help brush fat slabs of ribs with Thomas's secret recipe barbecue sauce, flour up chicken for frying, husk corn for boiling and peel potatoes for salad. Marnie had never seen so much food in her life. When she'd asked Jenna why they didn't just let caterers take care of everything, the other woman had looked horrified. Because, she'd told Marnie, that wasn't the way her mother had raised her—or Thomas's mother had raised him. When you invited people over for supper, you fixed them supper yourself.

When Marnie followed Daniel outside, balancing two big bowls of potato chips with a bowl of dip, she saw that the Prestons had hired a local bluegrass band to play and laid out a makeshift floor on a flat patch of ground for dancing. There were games and activities for the children of Quest's employees, one of those big plastic bouncy things that Marnie remembered loving when she was a kid, and—it went without saying— pony rides.

"Boy, not bad for a last-minute get-together," she told Daniel as they set their bowls down on one of a half-dozen tables set up for food and drink.

It was warmer today than it had been since Marnie's arrival, and the sun hung high and bright in the June sky.

She'd deferred to the heat by donning a pair of denim shorts and sandals, topped by a loose-fitting cropped T-shirt of pale blue. Daniel was wearing his standard blue jeans, but had dressed them up with a chocolate-brown polo that matched his eyes. As she watched him set two sweaty pitchers of iced tea on the table beside the chips, the warm breeze caught in his black hair and nudged a stray piece over his forehead. It was all she could do not to reach out and push it back again when he straightened and looked at her. Just as well, though, since he took care of that himself. Just the way he took care of everything himself, she couldn't help thinking.

He nodded as he surveyed the crowd. "Yeah, Tom is pretty amazing when it comes to organizing these things. The Prestons have at least one party this big every summer—though they usually take weeks to plan it, not hours. And they have a big fall get-together after the Keeneland auction in November, and a massive Derby party every spring."

"But this year, they were *at* the Derby," Marnie said.

"Every year, they're at the Derby," Daniel told her.

"You mean, they spring for a big party, and they're not even here?"

He shrugged. "They figure they shouldn't be the only ones having a good time Derby day. They want to keep their employees happy. Everyone at Quest makes the stable the success that it is. It's a team effort all the way, and the Prestons never forget that. And they don't want their employees to forget that they don't forget."

"They're nice people," Marnie said.

"The best," Daniel agreed.

"I can see why you like working here so much."

"Yeah, it's a pretty good gig." He hesitated a moment before adding, "For now."

She looked at him again, curiously this time. "You're not planning on making a career out of it?"

He said nothing for a moment, and judging by his expression, she got the feeling he was wishing he hadn't said as much as he had. Finally, though, he told her, "Not here at Quest, no. I still hope to have my own place one day. For now, though, this is about as good as it gets. Still…"

His voice trailed off without his finishing whatever he was going to say. "Still…what?" Marnie asked.

He sighed. "I don't know. I've just been feeling a little restless lately, that's all. My dad getting shot didn't help matters. Seeing him laid up like that, it reminded me that he's not as young as he used to be, and he's not going to be around forever." He sighed heavily. "I guess I'm just starting to feel the distance between him and me. And not just the geographic distance, either. He and I have never been that close, and I wonder if it isn't time one of us, anyway, addressed that."

Marnie was going to say something reassuring—though, honestly, he seemed so bothered at the moment that she wasn't sure he could be reassured—when a woman began singing with the bluegrass band, her voice melodious and powerful enough to drown out the chorus of cicadas that had been serenading them along with the musicians up to that point.

"Holy cow," Marnie said as she looked in the direction of the music.

"What?" Daniel asked.

"The woman singing with the band…" She gestured at the slim, girl-next-door blonde who was dressed in the sort of jeans one did *not* wear to work on a farm and a black Western-style shirt trimmed in silvery beads. "She looks and sounds just like Elizabeth Innis, the country music singer. In fact, she's singing Elizabeth Innis's latest hit single."

Daniel smiled. "That's because she is Elizabeth Innis. She's Thomas and Jenna's niece. Her mother is Jenna's sister."

"Wow," Marnie said, genuinely impressed. "I had no idea."

"And I had no idea you were a country fan," Daniel remarked. "You were always listening to that weird stuff in Del Mar."

"Alternative," she corrected him. "Not weird stuff. And I don't listen to country music that much. But Elizabeth Innis has had crossover success and she's on the radio a lot. I like what I've heard of her music."

Marnie waited for the stitch of sadness that always pricked her whenever one of them mentioned San Diego, but it never came. Strange, but she hadn't felt sad at all since coming to Kentucky. Even in light of the problems rocking the Prestons, there hadn't been a moment when she'd been overcome by the melancholy sensations that had dogged her in Hunter Valley after seeing Daniel again.

Probably, she thought, it was because she'd managed to keep herself busy since being here. That must be it. What other explanation could there be?

"You know, Elizabeth's not the only celebrity with ties to the Prestons and Quest," Daniel said. "Have you heard of Demetri Lucas?"

"The race car driver?" Marnie asked. She'd heard of him because he lived in California, as she did, and often showed up on the numerous celebrity-watch shows Marnie viewed religiously to keep track of what was going on in the world many of her clients lived in—and to stay on top of what some of her clients were doing themselves. She hated it when the paparazzi and report-ers knew about their mishaps before she did.

"That's him," Daniel said. "He's a friend of Hugh's. He owns several of the horses here at Quest."

Marnie looked out over the crowd again, quizzing herself on the names of the people she'd met so far besides the Prestons. She saw Melanie talking to her friend Julia Nash, a writer for *Equine Earth* magazine who had been a huge ally in the past few days, writing some wonderful articles about Quest that would be pub-lished soon. Near them Audrey was talking to Carter Phillips, Quest's veterinarian, who had been hit almost as hard by the news of Legacy's questionable paternity as the Prestons. Carter had supervised Legacy's breeding and brought the horse into the world and had as big a personal investment in the animal as he did professional.

In fact, Marnie thought as she surveyed the crowd,

just about everyone at Quest had a personal interest in the outcome. Daniel was right. This whole place was like one big family. Everyone knew everyone else, and everyone watched out for everyone else. It wasn't just their own kids Thomas and Jenna took care of. It was everyone who worked for Quest, in any capacity.

And now, in a way, Marnie was a part of that family, too. Even after having been here only a few days, she'd come to care about the Prestons and the people who worked for them more than she'd ever cared about the people she worked with back in San Diego. Like too many large corporations, Division International wasn't big on coworker camaraderie. There had been a lot of competition among her colleagues, and sometimes no cooperation. It had been a totally different environment from the one Daniel worked in.

She could see now why his work was such a big part of his life. But having heard him voice doubts about his relationship with his father, she couldn't help wondering if he still believed he didn't have room for anything—or anyone—else. Because if he was starting to have second thoughts about his relationship with his father, might he be having second thoughts about his relationships with other people? People like, oh, say… Marnie? And why did she find herself hoping he was? Hadn't she had her fill of being hurt by him? Why couldn't she just let him go?

Why, dammit, couldn't she stop loving Daniel Whittleson?

Chapter Twelve

Around the huge bonfire that always ended the Preston shindigs, the family's Irish heritage came to the surface, and the stories began.

It was Brent's daughter Rhea, Daniel noted, who started it by crawling into her grandfather's lap. "Tell us a story, Grandaddy."

"Yeah, Grandaddy," Katie agreed as she followed her sister into his lap, the two girls vying for position as Thomas laughed and helped get them settled. "Tell us about the time Great-Grandad came to the United States and met Great-Grandma and bought Old Barley and won the race that let him buy Quest, and—"

"Keep going, Rhea," Thomas gently interjected with

a chuckle, "and I won't have to tell the story, because you'll have already told it."

Hugh, who was seated next to Thomas, his Irish wolfhound at his feet, made a face. "Oh, come now, girls," he said, his voice still mellowed by his Irish accent. "You've heard that story a thousand times. Let your father tell a different one. Let him tell about the time he met your mother. I rather like that one meself."

"Noooo!" the girls chorused. "We want to hear about Great-Grandad!"

Thomas chuckled and gave his father an affectionate pat on the back. "Sorry, Dad, but they outnumber you."

"Those wee things?" Hugh said with a wink for the girls. "Why, they barely weigh as much as me little finger."

Thomas put his arms around both of his granddaughters, who by now each claimed a knee. Then he smiled, his expression warming to the one Daniel recognized as Irish Storyteller. Thomas may not have come from the Old Country like his father, but he felt his Irish roots as strongly. Thomas looked at Marnie when he spoke, Daniel noticed, probably because she was the only one in the group who hadn't heard the story.

"It all started in 1922," he began as he always did, "in a little thatched-roof farmhouse in County Clare. There on the Emerald Isle, among the green hills and gray skies and stony fences and fat bleating sheep, my father, Hugh Preston, was born, the youngest of six strapping Irish lads. Hugh learned two things growing up in the mother country—how to work with his bare hands from sunup to sundown and how to pick horses at the local stakes races."

A ripple of soft laughter went up among the guests, including Marnie. She sat close enough to the fire that her face was bathed in the golden glow and her cheeks were rosy with warmth. She leaned forward a little bit and propped her elbows on her knees, cradling her chin in both palms. Her auburn curls glistened in the firelight, taking on the same hue as the flames, first orange, then amber, then ocher, and Daniel had to battle an urge to lift a hand to her hair and tangle those curls around his fingers.

"Like any young man worth his salt," Thomas continued, "Hugh left home at eighteen to make his mark on the world. Like many of his countrymen, he crossed the Atlantic on a steamship and landed in New York City. There, he and two other good Irish lads shared a cold dingy flat in Brooklyn and began to work long hours on the docks for very little cash. But where many of his colleagues tried to better their situations through the unions, Hugh spent every extra moment he had at the track. He watched the horses and jockeys, and he talked to the trainers and exercisers, and eventually, he was placing penny-ante bets. And a curious thing about Hugh Preston. He never, ever, lost."

Thomas went on for some time after that, describing how Hugh bought his first filly, Clare's Quest, for whom the farm was named, and how he bought his first farm in upstate New York with the winnings from her first race and started a breeding program there. He told how his father met and married rich society girl Maggie Lochlain after selling her a horse from his first generation of colts, and how the young couple battled Maggie's parents' disapproval and threats of disinheritance. And about the two strapping sons Hugh and Maggie had— Thomas, and his younger brother, David. And about how one of their horses, Old Barley, finally hit big at Saratoga, enabling the Preston clan to buy a thousand acres in Kentucky that would become Quest Stables.

Thomas waxed less poetic when talking about himself and his brother, David. But he went on to describe how, with a hefty inheritance from Maggie's parents—with whom Maggie and Hugh eventually reconciled—David struck out on his own in the tradition of his grandfather and moved to Australia to open his own stables and marry Sarah Cambria, whose parents owned a nearby vineyard.

By the time Thomas finished the story, Katie and Rhea both had nodded off. Brent gathered one little girl in his arms to take her to bed, and Thomas followed with the other. The whole party began to break up after that. By unspoken mutual agreement, Daniel and Marnie rose as one and began to walk back to their cabins.

The moment they were away from the crowd, Daniel started to feel awkward. He told himself he shouldn't. It wasn't as if this was the first time he and Marnie had been alone, even since returning to Kentucky. But something had changed between them. Or maybe it had changed even before they'd left Australia. Maybe that was why he'd told Marnie what he had at Louisa's party about how important she'd become to him eight years ago.

If only Louisa hadn't interrupted them. If only things hadn't fallen apart with Legacy after that. If only the two of them could have had a chance to talk about whatever was happening in an environment that wasn't fraught with other problems.

If only, if only, if only…

Maybe that was why things felt awkward now, he thought. Because so many things between them were still so unsettled. During the day, they had the mystery of Leopold's Legacy to keep them occupied. But at night…

He sighed inwardly. Ah, the night.

Somehow, he sensed Marnie felt the awkwardness, too, because she didn't say a word as they walked along through the darkness. Clouds had rolled in just after sunset, obscuring the moon and stars, painting the night sky completely black. There was enough light from the big house and the remaining party lights for them to find their way, but they walked slowly, just in case. They arrived at Marnie's cabin first, and, like a boy bringing his date home from the prom, Daniel walked her to her door. He wasn't sure why. It just seemed like the right thing to do. Unfortunately, kissing her good-night suddenly felt like the right thing to do, too, and the last couple of times he'd felt like that, the situations had ended badly.

But the circumstances had been different those times, he reminded himself. He and Marnie had been embroiled in a volatile situation that had them on opposite sides. They weren't on opposite sides of anything now. In fact, they had a common goal in clearing up the mystery surrounding Legacy's paternity. And Daniel, at least, was thinking that that wasn't the only thing they should be working on together.

"Home sweet home," Marnie said as they came to a halt at her front door. "Thanks for making sure I got here safely," she added with a nervous smile. "This is such a questionable neighborhood."

Daniel smiled back. But he felt as anxious as she looked, and he couldn't help wondering if she was thinking the same thing he was. Namely, what would happen if he tried to kiss her this time.

"I think the barbecue was a big hit," he said, giving himself a mental kick for not being able to come up with anything more meaningful to say.

"Everyone seemed to have a good time," she agreed. "And it was fun hearing about Quest's beginnings."

Not sure what to say next, Daniel lifted a hand nervously to the back of his neck and sighed. "I guess I'll see you in the morning."

She nodded. "Guess so."

There was another awkward silence, then—

"Marnie, I—"

"Daniel, I—"

They spoke as one and halted as one, gazing at each other with great expectation.

"Go ahead," Daniel said when she made no move to finish.

She bit her lower lip anxiously, and it was all he could do not to lean in and nibble it himself. "I was just going to say, um, I had a nice time."

He was pretty sure that wasn't what she'd planned to say.

"Your turn," she said.

"I was just going to tell you I appreciate everything you're doing for the Prestons," he told her. Not exactly what he'd really wanted to say.

She nodded at that, looking as though she believed him about as much as he believed her. "No problem," she told him. "Hey, it's my job."

So it was. But somehow, he suspected that even if it wasn't, she'd still be helping them out. And not just because her job was more important to her than anything. She'd gotten awfully involved on a personal level with the Prestons. Could there possibly, maybe, be a chance she might include Daniel in that involvement, too?

Not tonight, evidently, because she took a step backward, closer to her door, and said, "Good night, Daniel. I'll see you tomorrow."

He lifted a hand in farewell. "Tomorrow," he told her. He opened his mouth to say something else, thought better of it and closed it again. Then, with one final Herculean effort, he spun on his heel and made his way back to his cabin. He heard the sound of Marnie's front door opening and closing as he walked, and something about it seemed so final.

No, not final, he told himself as he picked his way

carefully through the darkness. There was still something arcing between him and Marnie that was far from being settled.

He just wished he knew exactly what that something was.

For the week that followed the barbecue, Marnie was a veritable PR machine for the Prestons while the others tried to solve the mystery of Leopold's Legacy's paternity. They entertained every theory they could think of for the discrepancy—computer glitch, mix-up at the DNA lab, clerical error, even deliberate sabotage. Being a native Californian, Marnie cautioned them not to rule out El Niño, either. But none of their potential theories made any more sense than the others, and there was no solid evidence to support any of them.

Marnie barely saw Daniel during those days, because they were both too busy with Legacy-related duties, but there were times when they'd be working in the same room, and she would look up to find him watching her in a way that made her stomach pitch and her heart hammer harder and her breath catch in her throat. Because there was something in that look that reminded her of the way he had been with her in San Diego. For just the briefest of moments, in that split second before he realized she'd caught him staring at her, he was the Daniel she'd known eight years ago, the one who would, every now and then, let down his guard and show her the happy, hopeful human being beneath the cool, cautious career man. The one who had laughed with her and held hands with her and made such sweet, sensuous love to her.

The one with whom she had thought she was falling in love.

But the second he realized she was watching him, the curtain would come down again, and he would be the man for whom work was everything. The only thing. At least, the only thing that mattered. And, feeling a little prick of disappointment—disappointment and something more acute—Marnie would go back to work, too.

As hard as she had worked to make the Fairchild Gala a success and repair Louisa's standing in the community, Marnie worked even harder for the Prestons. The news of Leopold's Legacy's questionable paternity hit the Thoroughbred world hard, and the fallout was nothing short of atomic. Coming on the heels of the Belmont Stakes as it did, and coupled with Legacy's last-minute scratching from that race and his heartbreaking loss of a chance to win the Triple Crown, it was all anyone could talk about. Even people whose interest in Thoroughbred racing lasted only the weeks between the Derby and the Belmont were fascinated by the story.

But then, everybody loved a scandal.

And *scandal* was the word the press and everyone else had picked up and run with, despite the Prestons' efforts to call it something else. *Mystery. Error. Incongruity. Anomaly. Discrepancy.* All were words they'd emphasized whenever they spoke of the event, but none of those contributed to selling newspapers or airtime the way *scandal* did.

In spite of that, Marnie stayed focused on the matter at hand. She watched the media reports, talked to her contacts in the horse world and gathered all the facts she could to help her develop a strategy for Quest Stables. She worked her usual magic with her press releases, and commissioned stories about other aspects of Quest Stables that focused on all the good things going on— Melanie's blazing career as a woman jockey and young Robbie's gifts as a trainer of champions. Andrew's homegrown success with his MBA from the University of Kentucky. She even got Hugh Preston to give some interviews about Quest's beginnings, and he'd charmed the socks off every reporter who came around. And always, always, everyone involved made clear that they were doing whatever it took and sparing no expense to get to the bottom of the mystery.

For every negative story that was printed or aired about Legacy's shady beginnings and Quest's questionable character, Marnie fired back with three that cast the stable in a positive light. It was exhausting for everyone, but they knew it was necessary and persevered.

And then, a week after the story broke, Marnie hit pay dirt and landed a plum national television spot for the Prestons. Not a two- or three-minute sound bite, but an honest-to-goodness thirty-minute interview with one of the country's leading, and most beloved, network interviewers—Stella Hathaway. Her occasional evening interviews with celebrities were some of the most watched television on the networks, always landing in one of the top three slots of the Nielsen ratings whenever they aired. Stella was known for treating her subjects with respect and asking tough, but fair, questions.

Marnie was confident she would be the perfect interviewer for Jenna Preston. Two strong, intelligent, articulate women discussing in depth how something like this could have happened at any stable, how the Prestons had been as shocked and troubled by the discovery as anyone, and how hard they were all working to put everything to rights. Just by being her usual charming and likable self, Jenna would easily win the hearts and minds of America and show that the situation with Leopold's Legacy was *not* a scandal. It was a mystery. An error. An incongruity. An anomaly. A discrepancy.

The second Tuesday after Marnie went to work for the Prestons, Stella and her crew arrived at Quest Stables and proceeded to set up in the sunroom. The interview would be taped that evening, they'd been told, and air as the first half of a show the following Friday. Best of all, the second half of the show would feature an interview Stella had taped two days before with none other than George Clooney. Talk about a ratings bonanza. Soon the entire country would hear from the Preston matriarch herself that Quest Stables was still the honorable institution they'd come to know and trust, and that the Preston family was still acting with integrity, doing everything they could to solve the mystery of Leopold's Legacy.

Blond, blue-eyed, dainty-looking Stella was magnanimous when she introduced herself to everyone, with ready smiles and laughter, and a demeanor that immediately put everyone at ease. She'd dressed to look at home on a Thoroughbred farm—well, as at home as someone who had lived and worked in Manhattan for years could look on a Thoroughbred farm—in a pink Western-style blouse and designer jeans and expensively tooled cowboy boots that were probably fresh from the box. Her production crew had given Jenna some guidelines for her own attire, but had essentially asked her to wear whatever she would normally wear on a typical working day. So she'd dressed in tailored blue jeans and a dark red shirt, accessorizing them with a few long strands of multicolored beads and matching bracelet and earrings.

"I'm so nervous," she told Marnie as they and the rest of the family and Daniel watched preparations for the show. They were going to be shooting in the sunroom, because even this late in the day, there was so much natural light.

"Don't worry," Marnie said in her most soothing PR voice. "You'll be great. I've seen you on TV a lot this week, and the camera loves you."

"But what if Stella asks me questions I can't answer?"

"Not to worry," Marnie told her with a smile. "I gave them a list of preapproved questions, and they've agreed to abide by that list. There aren't any questions you haven't already answered." When Jenna still seemed fretful, Marnie patted her arm. "Don't worry," she said again, more adamantly. "Stella isn't one of those ambush journalists. And the two of you hit it off beautifully. In a few hours, we'll be toasting your glorious network debut with champagne. Which reminds me," she added, "I should go put that on ice right now."

Thomas leaned forward to kiss his wife on the cheek. "You're smart, you're beautiful, and you're going to do great. We'll probably have to hire someone to answer your fan mail after this."

Jenna blushed and swatted his hand. "Oh, shush. I just want to do right by Quest Stables."

"And you will," Thomas stated confidently.

Marnie was about to say more, but the production assistant lifted a hand to signal to Jenna that they were ready for her. Thomas kissed her once more for good luck, Daniel told her to break a leg, and her children gave her a quick group hug. Marnie threw her a thumbs-up as Jenna headed to the sofa they'd moved in front of a window that looked out on one of the Quest pastures. The crew had asked Thomas to release some of the horses there. A half dozen of them were grazing peacefully beyond the windows as the sun was just beginning to set, providing a breathtaking backdrop for the interview.

As Marnie watched Jenna and Stella get comfortable, she smiled with contentment and relief. This interview was going to go a long way toward showing the public what good people the Prestons were, what a respectable business Quest Stables was, how hard everyone was working to ensure that everything—everything—was going to be put to rights.

This interview was nothing short of a dream come true.

The interview was nothing short of a nightmare.

Two hours after it concluded, Daniel was still trying to figure out what had gone wrong. Stella Hathaway had savaged Jenna to the point where they all now referred to the interviewer as "Stella Hackaway." Because hack away at Jenna—and Jenna's character and credibility— was all Stella did for the thirty minutes that the two women were taping. Of course, none of them knew that until after it was over and Jenna came out of the sunroom in tears. And by then, the production crew was packing up.

According to Jenna, the interview had started off pleasantly enough. Stella had greeted her warmly and congratulated her on the stunning performance of Leopold's Legacy in the Derby and Preakness. But the pleasantries had ended there. Blond, blue-eyed, benign-looking Stella, who was so wholesome and sweet-looking that she'd been crowned Miss Kansas once upon a time, had used her congratulations as a spring-board for a merciless attack. Jenna told them Stella ignored the list of preapproved questions that Marnie had provided and instead launched an attack of unfair charges and snide insinuations. For whatever reason, Stella Hathaway had taken off the gloves and gone after her interview subject with a vengeance.

Daniel was betting that reason had something to do with Stella having lost a bundle at the track at Derby and Preakness.

As Jenna told them what happened, Thomas's anger had become almost palpable. But to Daniel's surprise, Marnie's was even greater. While Thomas did his best to comfort his wife, Marnie marched back into the sunroom and confronted both Stella and her producer, a tall dark-haired woman dressed completely in black. Susan something, Daniel recalled. Marnie started off with a furious "Just what the *hell* was that?" and ended with a livid "You have *not* heard the last from me *or* the Prestons' attorneys."

When she stomped back out to where the Prestons and Daniel were standing, he saw that she was literally shaking with anger. In spite of that, she lifted a comforting hand to Jenna's shoulder. "I *will* take care of this," she assured her client. "That interview will not go on the air. But let's all remember this incident and learn from it. The press isn't going to play fair, no matter how nice we try to be to them. It's going to take a lot more than a good PR campaign to handle this. I'll keep doing what I can, but things could get very ugly, and you should keep that in mind."

At midnight, Daniel and Marnie were both still wide-awake, sitting on the front porch of Marnie's cabin. He had stopped by his own place long enough to grab a bottle of Bourbon and two glasses, thinking they could both use a shot, and he'd poured one for each of them before folding himself into the Adirondack chair beside hers. The fact that she wasn't a Bourbon drinker hadn't deterred Marnie. She'd slugged back the first, flinched a little and held out her glass for a second. He'd taken a little more time with his first than she had, but he was working on number two himself. Funny, but neither of them seemed to be feeling the effects. Grief, shock and disbelief had a way of holding off the very things that were supposed to counter them.

"I still don't understand what went wrong," Marnie said. "Everyone on Stella's staff was so nice and cooperative when I set this up. They assured me the questions I gave them were perfect and that they'd stick to them. How could Stella have been so vicious to Jenna?"

"I don't know," Daniel said. "Maybe the network needed a ratings boost. These days, the term 'television journalism' is becoming an oxymoron. No one seems to want to report the facts anymore. They just want to sell commercials."

"Did you hear what the producer had the temerity to say to me?" Marnie invoked a self-important whine as she mimicked the other woman. "'We only report the news. We don't make it.'"

Yeah, right, they reported the news, Daniel thought distastefully. They reported the news as they wanted the world to see it, and that was with rumor, gossip and innuendo mixed together for the most pandering kind of sensationalism.

Marnie took another sip of her drink, flinching a bit

less this time. "I'm surprised Jenna and Thomas could even look at me after the interview was over."

"How can you say that?" he asked curiously.

She looked back at him. "Because I'm responsible for what happened, that's how."

"No, you aren't," he told her. "Stella Hathaway is responsible. She and her crew and the morons at the network who told her to go after Jenna with both guns drawn."

"But I'm the one who set up the interview," Marnie said. "I'm the PR person. It's my job to make sure things like this don't happen."

"Marnie, you did just what you were supposed to do. You set up a national interview to help out the Prestons and did everything within your power to make sure it went off well. No one blames you for any of this."

"I do," she said.

"Well, stop it."

She sighed heavily. "You know, ever since I went into PR, there have been times when I've wondered about what I do for a living. Don't get me wrong," she hastily added, "usually, I really enjoy it. But lately, so much of it makes me feel like I'm a handler for rich, pampered people who don't deserve and certainly haven't earned any of the nice things they have. When I finally got something worthwhile to do for decent, hardworking people like the Prestons, I blew it."

"Marnie, that isn't true. You yourself said you'll take care of this. That you'll make sure that interview never airs. That's not what I call blowing it."

"It *is* true, Daniel." She turned in her chair, and even in the darkness, he could see the distress in her expression. "Yes, I'll get that tape pulled from production completely, but the point is that it shouldn't be necessary in the first place. I shouldn't have to do damage control on the damage control. I should have done it right the first time."

She stood suddenly and ran a hand through her hair. "I really wanted to do a good job for the Prestons. Not just to help them, and not just because I didn't want to let them down, but because I wanted to prove to myself that there were some causes, and some people, worth spinning in a positive light."

"There *are* causes and people like that," he told her. He stood up, too. "Just because things didn't work out this time doesn't mean what you do for a living isn't important."

She shook her head and stared blindly out into the darkness.

"I just want to have meaning," she said. "I just want to feel like I contribute something worthwhile to the world, you know?"

"Oh, Marnie," he said, reaching out to her. "Don't you realize how meaningful you are? How much you do contribute? How important you've become? Not just to the Prestons, but to—" He halted before finishing, because he honestly wasn't sure how she would react to what he'd intended to say.

But when he looked at her and saw the way she was

looking back, something inside him turned over. "To who?" she asked softly.

"To me." He took a step forward to close what little distance lay between them and lifted his hand to tuck it under her hair. "You are so desperately needed here, Marnie. And it has nothing to do with your job."

Her voice was hesitant as she asked, "But who needs me the most, Daniel?"

"I do," he told her. "More than anything."

"Anything?" she echoed shallowly.

He nodded as he lowered his head to hers. "More than anything else in the world." And then, without thinking about anything other than that, he covered her mouth with his and kissed her.

Gently at first, tenderly, fearful on some level that she might put a stop to things as she had that first night in Hunter Valley. But she didn't. Instead, she turned her head a little and kissed him back. Just as gently, just as tenderly. Almost as if she'd been expecting him to do it, and very much as if she'd been wanting him to…

Chapter Thirteen

Marnie wasn't sure when her feelings changed from despondency over the outcome of the interview to desire for whatever was happening between her and Daniel. But it was the third time they'd come together since meeting again, and this time, she wasn't sure she had it in her to step back over the line where she told herself she belonged. Daniel had said he needed her. More than anything else in the world. Did that mean he loved her, too? That there was still a chance for them after all the time and words and emotions that had passed?

And then she stopped thinking at all, because what was going on in her heart was so much stronger than what was happening in her head, and those feelings were simply too good to tamp down. She only knew that one minute, she and Daniel were talking about the fate of Quest Stables, and the next, they were talking about their own, and somehow the two seemed irrevocably entwined, and she didn't want to leave any of it. Not Quest, not the Prestons, not Daniel.

Especially not Daniel. Oh, God, not ever again.

As he kissed her, he took her glass from her hand to set it next to his on the table between the Adirondack chairs. Then he pulled her into his arms more resolutely, opening his mouth against hers to taste her deeply. She felt his hands opening over her back, one skimming down her spine as the other curled more snugly around her nape to bury itself in her hair. So she lifted her hands, too, gliding her fingertips over his rough jaw, down his warm throat, over his hard shoulders, into his silky hair, savoring all the ways his body was different from her own and reveling in his maleness.

With each stroke of her fingers, he intensified the kiss, until he seemed to tower over her and his body surround her. Every time Marnie managed to take a breath, she was filled with the scent of him, every time she kissed him, her mouth was filled with the taste of him. His heart hammered against hers, the pulsing of each accelerating until they seemed to be beating as one. Even their breathing seemed to be in harmony— ragged, fierce harmony—as they kissed.

At some point, Marnie became vaguely aware that Daniel was pushing open the cabin's front door, then they were half walking, half pulling each other into the living room. He closed the door again with one foot, then they began the walking-pulling thing across the living room. With one hand tangled in her hair, he dragged the other down her back, inching lower until he curled his fingers over her fanny and pushed her body into his. Marnie responded instinctively, rubbing her pelvis against his, slowly, arduously, smiling at his answering groan of need. His other hand joined the first on her bottom, and he pushed harder, grinding himself into her waiting softness. This time Marnie was the one to groan in demand, dropping her hands to his taut buttocks and squeezing hard.

The kiss that followed nearly consumed her. As he kissed her, he bunched the fabric of her shirt in one fist and pushed it higher, until she felt the cool night air caressing her hot flesh. When his fingers had crept high enough for him to reach her bra, he unfastened it with one deft maneuver, then pushed it aside to open his hand wide over her naked skin.

Marnie had worked his shirt free of his blue jeans and skimmed her fingers lovingly over the sea of muscles that swelled on his back. Her other hand went to work on the buttons, pushing his shirt open when she was through, burying her fingers in the dark field of hair on his chest. He was hard in the places she was soft, rough in the places she was smooth. But his desire mirrored her own. He embraced her as fiercely as she did him, touched her as fervently as she touched him. They both wanted. They both needed. They both intended to have.

As if he'd read her mind, he found the button of her jeans, then deftly tugged down the zipper, a favor she immediately returned. Then his hands were at her back again, diving beneath both the denim and her panties to curve over her bare bottom, stroking her sensitive skin. She grew hotter and damper between her legs with every touch, then nearly shattered when he dipped one insistent finger into the delicate cleft of her behind.

"Oh," she murmured against his mouth. "Oh, Daniel…"

But he was kissing her again before she could say more, and pushing his finger harder against her, generating sensations that made speaking pretty much impossible.

As he continued to caress her, she moved herself far enough away from him so that she could push her hand into his blue jeans and cup the heavy length of him in her palm. He murmured a satisfied sound in response and hitched his hips forward, pushing himself more fully against her fingers, silently encouraging her to take more of him. Eagerly, she pushed his jeans open wider and dipped her hand deeper, to cover him more intimately. Naked flesh against naked flesh, the way he was touching her. As she rubbed her hand along his shaft, she marveled at the heat and strength and size of him, and her need for him soared.

For long moments, they only kissed and touched each other, their breathing and heart rates accelerating with every second. Marnie wasn't sure which one of them took the initiative to move, but finally, slowly, deliberately, they made their way across the bedroom. They stopped kissing long enough to look into each other's eyes, as if each wanted to make sure this was the right thing to do. Then, without a word, they moved to the side of the bed and pulled back the bedclothes.

Daniel drew her back against him, his hardness pressing against her backside, sparking a heat that shot through her like a rocket blast. He bent his head to nuzzle the curve where her neck and shoulder joined, and Marnie reached behind to weave her fingers into his hair. Daniel took advantage of her position to unbutton her shirt and open it, then scooped his hands under her loosened bra to cover both breasts.

As he brushed butterfly kisses along her neck and shoulder, he gently kneaded her tender flesh. Catching one nipple in the V of his index and middle fingers, he pushed his other hand lower, over her naked torso, dipping into her navel as he passed it. Then he nudged his hand into her panties, down to her damp center, and buried his fingers in the swollen folds of her flesh.

Marnie gasped at the sensation that shot through her, her fingers tightening in his hair. Palming her breast with one hand, he caressed her with the other—slow, firm, methodical strokes. She opened her legs wider, then went still as he stroked her, her ragged breathing the only sound in the room. Gradually, he began to move his fingers faster, dragging them one way, then another, then drawing erotic little circles. Finally, he touched the pad of his middle finger to her most sensitive spot. Marnie's orgasm came fast and furious, nearly rendering her insensate with the intensity of it. Somehow she managed to get her body turned around so she could kiss him. And kiss him. And kiss him.

Amid those kisses, they undressed each other completely, until they stood face-to-face. Smiling, his gaze never leaving hers, he sat on the edge of the bed and pulled her into his lap so that she was facing him with her legs straddling his. Looping an arm around her waist, he began to kiss her again, even more ravenously than before. She palmed the smooth head of his shaft, then began to stroke him, taking time and care to be thorough. Daniel, in turn, caressed the tender curves of her bottom, up and down and back again, mimicking the movement of her fingers on him and his tongue inside her mouth.

Eventually, she felt them falling slowly backward onto the bed, and he turned their bodies so that they were lying side by side, Marnie on her back and he half atop her. He kissed her jaw, her cheek, her temple, her forehead, then moved lower, to her throat, her collarbone, her breast. There, he flattened his tongue to lick her nipple, then sucked it deep into his mouth, stirring the fire inside her to greater heights. Marnie closed her legs around his and bucked against him, rubbing herself wantonly against his thigh, and groaning as another shudder of heat overcame her.

Sensing her turmoil, Daniel dipped his head lower, trailing more kisses over her abdomen. He gripped her hips and knelt on the floor beside the bed, pulling her forward to drape her legs over his shoulders. Then he ducked his head to taste her even more intimately, running his tongue enthusiastically over the damp flesh he had touched before. He lapped leisurely with his tongue, then dived deeper with the tip. He pushed his hands beneath her hips to lift her higher, penetrating her deeply with his finger as he feasted upon her, hungrily, thoroughly.

Another ribbon of pleasure began to unwind inside her, starting low in her center and spiraling outward, until she trembled with the exquisiteness of it. Sensing how close she was, Daniel stood, this time grasping an ankle in each hand. He parted her legs wide and pushed himself forward, burying himself inside her—deep, *deep* inside her. He withdrew almost completely, then thrust forward again, repeating the action over and over. Finally, he joined her on the bed, hooking her legs around his waist and lowering his body over hers. He braced both elbows on the mattress and bucked his hips against hers, going deeper with each new penetration. Marnie gripped his hard biceps as he thrust faster, opening her legs wider, until, as one, they cried out with the explosion that rocked them.

And then they clung to each other for long moments, shuddering with the last remnants of their response. When Daniel withdrew, it was to collapse on the bed beside Marnie. But he didn't go far. Lying on his belly, he kept one arm draped over her torso and arched the other over his head to tangle his fingers in her hair. She didn't want to stop touching him, either, opening her hand over his heart and settling her head against his shoulder.

"Wow," she said when she was able to manage speech. "Just like old times, huh?"

She felt him shake his head. "That was even better than old times."

He was right, she thought. Their lovemaking in San Diego had been every bit as urgent and intense and explosive, but there had been something else this time, something more, something that hadn't been there before. She wasn't sure what, and at the moment, she was too frazzled to think about it. But it had been different this time. Better. Nicer. More satisfying. More complete.

"Still think you're not needed here?" he asked.

His question sobered her, and she tilted her head back to look at him. "I don't know," she said honestly. "It depends on what I'm needed for. If it's just sex—"

"It's not just sex," he immediately interrupted, turning his head to look down at her. Then he sobered, too. "Unless that's all you want it to be. Unless your career is still more important to you than—"

"My career *is* important, Daniel," she said. "But it's never been most important. Not the way yours is to you."

"Was to me," he corrected her. "Past tense. I may not be the fastest learner on the planet, Marnie, but I can learn. About horses, about my father, about work, about…"

By the time his voice trailed off, her heart was hammering hard in her chest, full of hope. "Go on," she told him almost breathlessly.

"About you," he finished softly. "About us. And once I learn something, Marnie, I make the most of it." He smiled at her then. "Like you said. I'm the best at what I do."

"And just what is it you're doing now?" she asked.

His fingers tightened in her hair. "Marnie, the man who left you in Del Mar, the man who thought his work was more important to him than anything…" He sighed heavily. "He's not the man lying here now. That guy… That guy didn't know what the hell he wanted. He thought the only way to be important was to do things people talk about. He thought the only way to have meaning was to be the best at something. Now I know the way to be important and meaningful is to love someone who loves me back. To share a life with someone *I* think is important. So what I'm doing now is loving you. Or maybe I'm finally realizing that I've loved you all along. And that I will go on loving you forever. I've finally realized it wasn't having you in my life that week before the race that distracted me and kept me from being my best. It was my fear of losing you. Of finally finding the one person in the world I could love forever, and then being afraid she might not love me the same way. But if I knew you'd be around forever…"

Something massive and fluid rushed through her at hearing his words, and Marnie realized it was the love she had always felt for him. There was so much of it, and it was so powerful, she feared for a moment it might consume her. Then she decided that consumption might not be such a bad thing. As long as Daniel was consumed alongside her.

When she said nothing, his smile fell some. "It's too little too late, isn't it?" he said fearfully. "You've spent the last five years building your career, and now you're at a point where you don't want to mess with it. It's more important to you than anything, isn't it? You don't have room for me or anyone else in there. Oh, God, I blew it, didn't I? I never should have—"

She lifted a hand and lightly covered his mouth. "You didn't blow it," she said with a smile. "I love you, too, Daniel. I think I always have. I know I always will. No matter what kind of career I have."

He expelled an unmistakable sigh of relief, caught her hand in his and pressed his fingers to her mouth. "Thank you for giving me a second chance," he murmured.

She lifted her other hand to his hair and sifted the strands through her fingers. Then she folded her body into his and brushed her lips along his warm shoulder. "You're welcome," she told him. "Sometimes, when something's very important, it takes a couple of tries to get it right."

He smiled down at her. "So then maybe we should… you know…" He covered her breast with his hand and raked his thumb playfully across her nipple, sending a bolt of heat through her entire system. "…a second time."

Marnie laughed and dropped her hand between his legs, where he was already coming to life. He was right, she thought as she closed her fingers around him. And there were some jobs she didn't mind putting first.

Instead of the Stella Hathaway interview that was supposed to have aired Friday night, the network broadcast a sixty-minute "introspective" of Hugh Preston and the amazing Thoroughbred legacy he began in New York and brought to Kentucky. The interviewer, Marnie Roberts, was a newcomer to broadcast television, but she did an excellent job of presenting both the man and his farm in Kentucky in a way that personalized both and charmed viewers. Unfortunately, the show aired opposite the network premiere of a theatrical blockbuster on another channel, so the ratings probably weren't as high as they would have been if, oh, say…someone had done a scandal-ridden ambush interview with a sweet-natured Jenna Preston. But the PR from the show was still overwhelmingly positive.

The atmosphere at the Preston house immediately following the broadcast was even better. The entire family plus Marnie and Daniel had gathered at the big house to watch, and as the credits rolled at the end, all of them applauded. Not just for Hugh, but for Marnie, too. For getting the job done.

"I don't know how you did it, Marnie," Thomas said as he switched off the TV and returned to his seat on the couch. "But that was some lemonade you made out of those Stella Hackaway lemons."

Marnie snuggled closer to Daniel on the sofa and

hoped her smile wasn't too smug. "It's amazing what a few words said to the right people can do."

Jenna smiled back. "And just what words did you say? And to which people?"

Marnie buffed her fingernails on the gray T-shirt emblazoned with the Quest Stables logo that the Prestons had given her, and which she'd paired with blue jeans and hiking boots. "I can't remember exactly," she fibbed modestly. "But I do recall the terms *defamation, libel* and *lawsuit* coming up. And I do remember one very panicky-sounding producer. Especially after I uncovered all those gambling debts of Stella Hackaway's. Who knew America's sweetheart reporter would owe so much money to so many racetracks? I mean, the money she lost on the Derby and Preakness alone could feed a small nation."

Jenna sighed. "Hopefully this is the wake-up call she needs to get some help."

Unbelievable, Marnie thought. Even after the way Stella had treated her, Jenna still wanted the best for her.

Daniel looped an arm around Marnie's shoulder and pulled her closer still. "All that matters is that everything worked out for the best."

Jenna nodded. "At least in terms of the interview. We've still got a long way to go before the mystery of Legacy's paternity is solved."

Thomas moved behind her chair and cupped his hands lovingly over her shoulders. "We'll get it straightened out, Jenna."

"Thank goodness we have Marnie to help," she said, smiling at Marnie. "We're lucky Daniel knew you."

Daniel smiled, too. "I'm the one who's lucky," he said. He was about to say more when the cell phone fastened to his blue jeans rang. He unhooked it and said hello, and almost immediately, his smile fell. Marnie only heard one side of the conversation, but that was in no way revealing. Mostly Daniel murmured some uh-huhs and uh-uhs and I sees. By the time he folded the phone closed again, his expression was grim.

"What is it?" Marnie asked.

He lifted his hand to the back of his neck and rubbed hard, a gesture Marnie had come to realize meant he was anxious about something. "It's my father," he said.

Marnie sat up straighter on the sofa. "Is he okay?"

"He's back in the hospital with an infection."

"Oh, no."

A ripple of concerned murmurs went through the family.

"He'll be okay," Daniel hurried to reassure them, "but it's a setback he doesn't need. On top of that, the nurse I hired to take care of him had to quit suddenly, without notice, to tend to her own father." He looked at Jenna and Thomas. "I really need to go back to Australia."

"Of course you do," Jenna agreed. "You'll leave right away."

He glanced from Jenna to Thomas, then at Marnie, then back to Thomas again. "Indefinitely," he added. "I think I really need to be with my father now, and I don't know for how long."

"That's fine, Daniel," Thomas assured him. "Take as long as you need."

Daniel looked at Marnie again. "Actually, it might be a permanent move," he said. He turned his attention to the Prestons again. "I've been thinking about leaving Quest for a while now. I love it here," he hastened to add, "but—"

"But it's not what you want to be doing forever," Thomas finished for him with a rueful smile. "I knew this day would come, Daniel. You're too good a trainer not to strike out on your own someday. But I confess I wish we could have had you a little while longer."

"I'm sorry to leave you in the lurch," Daniel told him. "Under other circumstances, I could have given you more notice so you could put another head trainer in place—"

"I could take over that position," Robbie piped up. "I'm ready. Look how well I've done with Legacy."

Thomas and Jenna exchanged a meaningful look, then Thomas told his youngest son, "We can talk about this later, Robbie."

"I'm ready," Robbie repeated.

Thomas's mouth flattened into a tight line. This was obviously something he and his son had already talked about, Marnie thought. And judging by the look of it, the talk hadn't gone well.

Her heart had dropped to her stomach at Daniel's announcement, and now it began to hammer hard. But it wasn't because Daniel might be moving halfway around the world. It was because she was afraid he might be intending to go alone.

As if reading her thoughts, he said, "Any chance you might be able to get away from work for a while and join me?"

Hope swelled inside her now, making her smile. "I don't know," she said. "I guess it depends."

"On what?"

"On just how long this leave of absence is going to be."

He arched that single dark brow that made heat seep through her. "Well, this is just a rough estimate," he said, "but maybe…sixty years? Seventy? I guess it all depends on what kind of strides medical science makes toward extending human life." He dipped his head to hers and kissed her lightly on the nose. "'Cause this human, Marnie, would like to spend as many years of his life with you as he can."

The hope that had been building inside her broke free then, rushing through her like a warm, effervescent river. "Why, Daniel Whittleson," she said playfully, "is this a proposal?"

"Only if you're planning to say yes," he told her.

"Yes," she replied immediately…amid the applause of everyone present.

She blushed, having genuinely forgotten the others were there, so focused had she been on Daniel. And when she ducked her head shyly into his shoulder, everyone in the room only clapped harder. Then the

Prestons circled Marnie and Daniel with congratulations and good wishes, and all of them promised to come to the wedding, no matter when or where it was.

"But, Daniel," Thomas said when the laughter quieted down, "what will you do in Australia? Work for your dad? Or will you go ahead and fly solo?"

Daniel shook his head. "I won't be ready to fly solo until my life settles down some. I want to focus on my dad—" he turned to smile at Marnie "—and my wife for a while before I try to go it alone. But I don't think Dad wants me working that closely with him. I'll try to find work at one of the other farms in Hunter Valley. I don't think I'll have a problem."

"Any farm would be lucky to get you," Marnie said.

He grinned at her again. "Like I said. I'm the lucky one. Lucky to have you."

She opened her palm over his rough cheek. "You do have me," she said. "Mind and body, heart and soul."

"It's only fair," he said, pulling her close, "since that's what you have of me, too."

He kissed her temple and settled his head against hers as Marnie snuggled as close to him as she could. As everyone else talked around her and Daniel, she sat silently, enjoying the feeling of being so close to him, in so many ways, and reveling in the knowledge that neither of them would ever be going anywhere again.

Well, except to Australia. Where, Marnie was sure, they would live happily ever after.

Epilogue

Daniel stood behind the main house of Lochlain Racing in Hunter Valley, sipping a postdinner coffee and enjoying the late-June sunset. He'd gone from summer to winter, from Northern Hemisphere to Southern, from single man to engaged. His fiancée— he still smiled when he thought of Marnie that way— was setting up her own PR firm in Hunter Valley. She intended to take on only clients whose causes she respected, and her first had already signed on: Louisa Fairchild. The old woman had stopped in to see Marnie as soon as she heard her former PR rep was back in town, and apologized for reacting the way she had that night at the gala. After the two women had talked a bit more, Louisa had told Marnie that if there was anything she could do to make up for causing her to lose her job, Louisa wanted to do it. Marnie had offered her a contract, and Louisa had signed on the spot.

Daniel turned his gaze upward, noting that even the sky above Lochlain wasn't the same sky that arced above Quest Stables. But some things, he thought as he watched the last of the evening sun spill over the gently rolling hills, never changed at all. The horses running through a distant field were as graceful and beautiful as the ones back home. One of those horses, Lightning Chaser, was especially intriguing. It was the one who had been awarded the Queensland Stakes win after Daniel's father's horse was disqualified. Even with that history, Daniel was excited to be training the animal. He was beginning to think Lightning might just be one of those horses that came along once in a lifetime.

It hadn't been easy explaining to his father why he was taking the job at Lochlain, considering the bad feelings between Sam and Tyler Preston. In the long run, though, his father had had no choice but to see the offer of head trainer as the excellent opportunity it was, and he'd grudgingly given his blessing. Sam was even coming around to the idea of mending relations with Tyler Preston, though Daniel knew it was going to take some time before the two men were completely comfortable around each other again.

He was just glad to be here, glad to be…home. Not just because Australia was his birthplace, but because he was here with Marnie, and there was nothing else in the world he could possibly want.

"I wanted to tell you goodbye."

Daniel spun around at the sound of the voice to find Marcus Vasquez, one of Lochlain's trainers—correction, one of Lochlain's *former* trainers—standing behind him. When Daniel had approached Tyler Preston about a position here, Tyler had enthusiastically taken him on, having lost his head trainer some months earlier. But Tyler had added a stipulation. He'd asked Daniel to put in a good word for Marcus with the Kentuckian Prestons, to see if they might be able to find a place for him there, because he wasn't reaching his potential at Lochlain and could offer more to a larger farm. After Daniel had spoken to Marcus and watched him in action, he'd been so impressed with the man, he'd told Thomas and Jenna he'd found his own replacement. He hadn't just recommended they offer a job to Marcus—he'd told them they'd be nuts if they didn't make him their new head trainer.

Sure, Marcus was still a little rough around the edges in some aspects. But a more gifted horseman—other than himself, of course—Daniel had never met. Now Marcus was set to leave for Kentucky, embarking on what Daniel hoped would be as good a change for him as this one was promising to be for Daniel.

"All ready to go?" he asked Marcus.

Marcus nodded. "As ready as I'll ever be. Thanks again for helping me get the position in Kentucky. I appreciate it."

"No problem. The Prestons are looking forward to having you start."

Daniel didn't know much about Marcus beyond what he'd observed himself and what Tyler had told him. That he'd grown up in Spain and had first worked with horses as a stable boy, and that, like Daniel, he'd worked in several countries besides Australia. Marcus didn't talk about himself, and Daniel sensed that was by design, not accident. His Hispanic heritage was clear in his black hair and brown eyes and olive complexion. He wasn't quick with smiles—except, Daniel had noted, when he was with the horses—and he had something of an unrefined demeanor. But he was a hard worker and took his training of champions seriously.

Maybe a little too seriously, Daniel thought. But that was something the man was going to have to learn for himself. The same way Daniel had.

"You're going to be fine," he told Marcus. "Everyone at Quest is pretty easygoing, and it's a great place to work."

Marcus nodded. "I'm not worried about that."

"You seem worried about something."

Marcus lifted a shoulder and let it drop. "But not that."

Daniel started to ask more, then thought better of it. Marcus wasn't secretive, but neither was he gregarious. There was something of a mystery hanging about the man, but it wasn't Daniel's place to try to solve it. He'd had his fill of mysteries, thanks to his experiences with Leopold's Legacy this month. Mysteries that were no closer to being solved now than they'd been when he'd left Quest a week ago. But those mysteries were for someone else to explore. Daniel only wanted one thing now. To get on with his life. Here in Australia, with Marnie. Where they would weather together whatever life brought.

And where they would never leave each other's side.

* * * * *

*Don't miss the other Thoroughbred Legacy
novels available this month:*

*BIDING HER TIME by Wendy Warren
PICTURE OF PERFECTION by Kristin Gabriel
SOMETHING TO TALK ABOUT by Joanne Rock*

*Follow the rest of the Legacy!
Coming in September 2008:*

*MILLIONS TO SPARE by Barbara Dunlop
COURTING DISASTER by Kathleen O'Reilly
WHO'S CHEATIN' WHO? By Maggie Price
A LADY'S LUCK by Ken Casper*

Coming in December 2008:

*DARCI'S PRIDE by Jenna Mills
BREAKING FREE by Loreth Anne White
AN INDECENT PROPOSAL by Margot Early
THE SECRET HEIRESS by Bethany Campbell*

*Ladies, start your engines with a sneak preview
of Harlequin's officially licensed
NASCAR® romance series.*

Life in a famous racing family comes at a price.

All his life Larry Grosso has lived in the shadow
of his well-known racing family—but it's now
time for him to take what he wants. And on top of
that list is Crystal Hayes—breathtaking,
sweet…and twenty-two years younger. But their
age difference is creating animosity within their
families, and suddenly their romance is the talk of
the entire NASCAR circuit!

*Turn the page for a sneak preview of
OVERHEATED
by Barbara Dunlop
On sale July 29 wherever books are sold.*

Rufus, as Crystal Hayes had decided to call the black Lab, slept soundly on the soft seat even as she maneuvered the Softco truck in front of the Dean Grosso garage. Engines fired through the open bay doors, compressors clacked and impact tools whined as the teams tweaked their race cars in preparation for qualifying at the third race in Charlotte.

As always when she visited the garage area, Crystal experienced a vicarious thrill, watching the technicians' meticulous, last-minute preparations. As the daughter of a machinist, she understood the difference a fraction of a degree or a thousandth of an inch could make in the performance of a race car.

She muscled the driver's door shut behind her and waved hello to a couple of familiar crew members in their white-and-pale-blue jumpsuits. Then she rounded the back of the truck and rolled up the door. Inside, five boxes were marked Cargill Motors.

One of them was big and heavy, and it had slid

forward a few feet, probably when she'd braked to make the narrow parking lot entrance. So she pushed up the sleeves of her canary-yellow T-shirt, then stretched forward to reach the box. A couple of catcalls came her way as her faded blue jeans tightened across her rear end. But she knew they were good-natured, and she simply ignored them.

She dragged the box toward her over the gritty metal floor.

"Let me give you a hand with that," a deep, melodious voice rumbled in her ear.

"I can manage," she responded crisply, not wanting to engage with any of the catcallers.

Here in the garage, the last thing she needed was one of the guys treating her as if she was something other than, well, one of the guys.

She'd learned long ago there was something about her that made men toss out pickup lines like parade candy. And she'd been around race crews long enough to know she needed to behave like a buddy, not a potential date.

She piled the smaller boxes on top of the large one.

"It looks heavy," said the voice.

"I'm tough," she assured him as she scooped the pile into her arms.

He didn't move away, so she turned her head to subject him to a *back off* stare. But she found herself staring into a compelling pair of green…no, brown…no, hazel eyes. She did a double take as they seemed to twinkle, multicolored, under the garage lights.

The man insistently held out his hands for the boxes. There was a dignity in his tone and little crinkles around his eyes that hinted at wisdom. There wasn't a single sign of flirtation in his expression, but Crystal was still cautious.

"You know I'm being paid to move this, right?" she asked him.

"That doesn't mean I can't be a gentleman."

Somebody whistled from a workbench. "Go, Professor Larry."

The man named Larry tossed a "Back off" over his shoulder. Then he turned to Crystal. "Sorry about that."

"Are you for real?" she asked, growing uncomfortable with the attention they were drawing. The last thing she needed was some latter-day Sir Galahad defending her honor at the track.

He quirked a dark eyebrow in a question.

"I mean," she elaborated, "you don't need to worry. I've been fending off the wolves since I was seventeen."

"Doesn't make it right," he countered, attempting to lift the boxes from her hands.

She jerked back. "You're not making it any easier."

He frowned.

"You carry this box, and they start thinking of me as a girl."

Professor Larry dipped his gaze to take in the curves of her figure. "Hate to tell you this," he said, a little twinkle coming into those multifaceted eyes.

Something about his look made her shiver inside. It

was a ridiculous reaction. Guys had given her the once-over a million times. She'd learned long ago to ignore it.

"Odds are," Larry continued, a teasing drawl in his tone, "they already have."

She turned pointedly away, boxes in hand as she marched across the floor. She could feel him watching her from behind.

* * * * *

*Crystal Hayes could do without her looks,
men obsessed with her looks, and guys who think
they're God's gift to the ladies.
Would Larry be the one guy who could blow all
of Crystal's preconceptions away?
Look for OVERHEATED
by Barbara Dunlop.
On sale July 29, 2008.*

Thoroughbred Legacy

The purse is set and the stakes are high…
Romance, Scandal and Glamour set in the
exhilarating world of horse-racing!

The Legacy Continues with Book #2

BIDING HER TIME

by Wendy Warren

When blacksmith-turned-wine hostess Audrey Griffin discovers
a fiery attraction with vintner Shane Preston, she's determined
to enjoy a no-strings-attached relationship. But something about
Audrey makes Shane want much more—despite the fact that
commitment leaves Audrey all shaky. Is she balking at love…
or simply biding her time?

*Look for BIDING HER TIME
in July 2008 wherever books are sold.*

SPECIAL EDITION

Kate's Boys

A late-night walk on the beach resulted in Trevor Marlowe's heroic rescue of a drowning woman. He took the amnesia victim in and dubbed her Venus, for the goddess who'd emerged from the sea. It looked as if she might be his goddess of love, too…until her former fiancé showed up on Trevor's doorstep.

Don't miss

THE BRIDE WITH NO NAME

by *USA TODAY* bestselling author

MARIE FERRARELLA

*Available August
wherever you buy books.*

Harlequin® Historical
Historical Romantic Adventure!

From *USA TODAY*
bestselling author
Margaret Moore

A LOVER'S KISS

A Frenchwoman in London,
Juliette Bergerine is unexpectedly
thrown together in hiding with
Sir Douglas Drury. As lust and
desire give way to deeper emotions,
how will Juliette react on discovering
that her brother was murdered—
by Drury!

*Available September
wherever you buy books.*

REQUEST YOUR FREE BOOKS!

2 FREE NOVELS PLUS 2 FREE GIFTS!

SPECIAL EDITION®

Life, Love and Family!

YES! Please send me 2 FREE Silhouette Special Edition® novels and my 2 FREE gifts (gifts are worth about $10). After receiving them, if I don't wish to receive any more books, I can return the shipping statement marked "cancel." If I don't cancel, I will receive 6 brand-new novels every month and be billed just $4.24 per book in the U.S. or $4.99 per book in Canada, plus 25¢ shipping and handling per book and applicable taxes, if any*. That's a savings of at least 15% off the cover price! I understand that accepting the 2 free books and gifts places me under no obligation to buy anything. I can always return a shipment and cancel at any time. Even if I never buy another book from Silhouette, the two free books and gifts are mine to keep forever.

235 SDN EEYU 335 SDN EEY6

Name	(PLEASE PRINT)
Address	Apt. #
City	State/Prov.	Zip/Postal Code

Signature (if under 18, a parent or guardian must sign)

Mail to the **Silhouette Reader Service:**
IN U.S.A.: P.O. Box 1867, Buffalo, NY 14240-1867
IN CANADA: P.O. Box 609, Fort Erie, Ontario L2A 5X3

Not valid to current subscribers of Silhouette Special Edition books.

Want to try two free books from another line?
Call 1-800-873-8635 or visit www.morefreebooks.com.

* Terms and prices subject to change without notice. N.Y. residents add applicable sales tax. Canadian residents will be charged applicable provincial taxes and GST. Offer not valid in Quebec. This offer is limited to one order per household. All orders subject to approval. Credit or debit balances in a customer's account(s) may be offset by any other outstanding balance owed by or to the customer. Please allow 4 to 6 weeks for delivery. Offer available while quantities last.

Your Privacy: Silhouette is committed to protecting your privacy. Our Privacy Policy is available online at www.eHarlequin.com or upon request from the Reader Service. From time to time we make our lists of customers available to reputable third parties who may have a product or service of interest to you. If you would prefer we not share your name and address, please check here. ☐

SSE08R

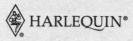

HARLEQUIN®

American ★ Romance®

MARIN THOMAS
A Coal Miner's Wife
HEARTS OF APPALACHIA

High-school dropout and recently widowed
Annie McKee has twin boys to raise. The
now single mom is torn between choosing
charity from her Appalachian clan or leaving
Heather's Hollow and finding a better future
for her boys. But her handsome neighbor and
deceased husband's best friend is determined
to show the proud widow there's nothing
secondhand about love!

Available August
wherever books are sold.

LOVE, HOME & HAPPINESS

www.eHarlequin.com   HAR75228

Silhouette®

SPECIAL EDITION™

NEW YORK TIMES BESTSELLING AUTHOR

DIANA PALMER

A brand-new Long, Tall Texans novel

HEART OF STONE

Feeling unwanted and unloved, Keely returns to Jacobsville and to Boone Sinclair, a rancher troubled by his own past. Boone has always seemed reserved, but now Keely discovers a sensuality with him that quickly turns to love. Can they each see past their own scars to let love in?

Available September 2008 wherever you buy books.